The Price of Friendship

by
Anne Schraff

Perfection Learning® Corporation
Logan, Iowa 51546

Editor: Pegi Bevins
Cover Illustration: Doug Knutson
Cover Design: Deborah Lea Bell

For Information, contact
Perfection Learning® Corporation
1000 North Second Avenue, P.O. Box 500
Logan, Iowa 51546-1099.
Tel: 1-800-831-4190 • Fax: 1-712-644-2392

Paperback ISBN 0-7891-5375-0
Cover Craft® ISBN 0-7807-9745-0
Printed in the U.S.A.
4 5 6 7 8 9 PP 08 07 06 05 04 03

1 Kirk shifted nervously in his seat. Mr. Ha was passing out the algebra tests the class had taken the day before.

"Here comes nothing!" B. J. Allen, one of Kirk's friends, muttered.

Kirk looked around at B. J., who sat behind him. No wonder he's worried, Kirk thought. He misses a lot of school. That makes it impossible to keep up.

Mr. Ha walked up and down the rows of desks. He handed a paper with a red score on it to each student.

"Oh, man," Roell Thompson, another of Kirk's friends, groaned when he saw his paper. From the sound of his groan, Kirk assumed he had not done very well.

"No way!" Desmond Brady protested. "I couldn't have done this bad." He covered his face with his hands and sighed.

Kirk winced when he caught sight of the F on B. J.'s paper. B. J.'s moan joined the chorus of others from the rest of the class.

When Kirk got his own test, he barely glanced at it. Then he quickly folded it in half and stuffed it into his algebra book.

"What did you get, Howie?" B. J. asked. Howie was short for Howell, Kirk's last name.

Kirk didn't want to tell his friend what he thought he had seen. "What do you think?" he shot back, hoping B. J. wouldn't press him for an answer.

But B. J. was thinking about his own grade. "Oh, man, my old man's going to be on my case about this," he sighed.

Kirk turned his attention to Mr. Ha, who was done passing out the tests. The Asian teacher was scolding his students in his gentle voice.

"When you don't turn in your daily work, I cannot correct your mistakes," he began. "If I don't know what you're doing wrong, *you* don't know what you're doing wrong. And those mistakes appear on your tests. And you know what that means—low test scores every time. In order to get good grades on your tests, it is imperative that you turn in your daily work. It's the only way. Right now, only a few of you are doing your daily work faithfully. The rest of you *must* put forth more effort."

Kirk knew he was one of the few faithful ones Mr. Ha was talking about. Kirk never failed to turn in his homework. It had been his dream since he was seven or eight to become an engineer. He wanted to build soaring bridges and looping freeways. He wanted to design buildings that glittered with glass and steel.

Kirk worked hard in all his classes, but math was most important to him. Math was the foundation of the career he had chosen.

Now, when Kirk was sure nobody was looking, he carefully opened his algebra book to take another look at his test. He wanted to make sure he'd seen the grade correctly. Ninety-eight points! Mr. Ha had drawn a big, red A and written "EXCELLENT!" beneath the score.

Kirk closed the book, joy welling up inside him. He knew that each time he got a good grade on a math test, he got a little closer to becoming an engineer. But he couldn't let B. J. see what he'd gotten. B. J. was one of Kirk's best friends. His other best friend was Tucker Chandler. The three boys had been inseparable since early childhood. Now they got together several times a week to shoot baskets or just hang out.

Kirk was like his two friends in many ways. All three were tall and loved basketball and rap music. When they got together, everything seemed funny. Kirk never laughed so hard as when he was with B. J. and Tucker.

But Kirk was different from his friends too. He had dreams of going to college and having a good career. He wanted to accomplish something in life—to be somebody.

Kirk remembered when B. J. had a dream. B. J. wanted to play professional basketball. His parents had encouraged him in his dream. But B. J.'s mother had died of cancer several years ago. And Mr. Allen's new wife made it plain that she wasn't crazy about having a teenage boy in the house. B. J.'s father was so desperately trying to please his new bride that he no longer gave any thought to his son's dreams.

Tucker Chandler, Kirk's other friend, had never really had any dreams. He had lost both parents to cocaine abuse before he was ten. Then he was sent to a series of foster homes where he never really fit in. He was too boisterous, too free-spirited, the social worker said. Various foster parents cared for Tucker without really *caring* for him. But Tucker hungered for a family. For a while it seemed as if his grandmother might take him in. But then she decided she was too old to handle a boy his age.

That was when B. J. and Kirk became the closest thing Tucker had to a family. He would often be at Kirk's house, and Kirk's mom would love him up as if he were her own child. Mrs. Howell always had enough love for everybody. B. J.'s mother did the same thing. But then Mrs. Allen died, and Kirk's mother became disabled. So Tucker didn't come around as much. By the time he was 14, he had a rap sheet for vandalism and fighting. And he was no longer a lonely little boy looking for love. He was well over six feet tall and was learning the ways of the streets. He dropped out of school, and not long after that, he joined the Red Princes, or Reps.

The Reps was a local gang made up mostly of dropouts from Garrison High. Kirk sometimes wondered if the Reps stationed a member outside the school just to recruit the kids who walked through the doors for the last time. It seemed that sooner or later all dropouts ended up in the Reps.

Since Tucker had become a Rep, he had been trying to talk Kirk and B. J. into dropping out and joining. B. J. had seriously considered it. But Kirk had no intentions of doing so. He was going to get all he could from high school and go on to become an engineer. Unfortunately, his attitude often came between him and his friends.

"You're starting to act white, Howie," Tucker would often accuse. "You're always studying. And for what? No matter how hard we work, we brothers aren't going anywhere except by our own wits, okay?"

"Tuck's got a point," B. J. said. "How many black faces do you see when they show the guys on Wall Street working at the stock market? You think there's a lot of black executives out there?"

"Yeah, and look at Garrison High," Tucker said. "How many black teachers do we have? We have whites and a few Asians. And we even have teachers from Saudi Arabia and Kuwait. But there's only two black teachers in the whole school. And Miss Hogan is trying so hard to pass for white that she doesn't even count. All we have is Mrs. Barnes, the music teacher. That's it. Am I right?"

"Yeah, got to have a black music teacher for all us kids who got rhythm!" B. J. added scornfully.

Tucker and B. J. had laughed bitterly at that.

After math class, B. J. and Kirk walked out together. "I'm getting closer and closer to thinking that Tuck's got the right idea," B. J. said. "I might as well drop out of this joint. Why do I come here every day just to get shamed by the teachers?"

Kirk wanted to tell B. J. that the teachers weren't shaming him. Any shame B. J. felt he brought on himself. But he didn't want to act like he was lecturing his friend. Instead he made the plea he had made so often. "Don't drop out, man. We're seniors.

We've stuck it out this long. A few more months and we're out of here—with a diploma. And that means a lot."

B. J. just shrugged and didn't answer.

Just then, a blond kid named Chad Spencer came by. Like Kirk, Chad planned on becoming an engineer. "Are you still interested in the chess club, Kirk?" he asked. "There's a meeting at noon today in room 216."

"Uh, thanks," Kirk said, avoiding B. J.'s eyes. He could see his friend staring at him in surprise. He hadn't told anyone about his passion for chess. He had discovered it quite by accident.

One day after school, he was doing research in the library when some of the chess club members came in. They set up several boards and started playing. One of them, Chad Spencer, had offered to teach Kirk how to play. In no time, Kirk was hooked on the challenging game. He discovered that it took logical thinking and planning—just the kinds of things he'd have to do as an engineer.

"See you there," Chad said, moving on.

"Chess?" B. J. cried when Chad was out of

earshot. He bent over laughing, holding his sides. "What has that dude been smoking? He thinks a brother wants to sit at a little table and move funny little wooden pieces around! That's a fool's game."

"Uh, actually, it's kind of fun, B. J.," Kirk said. "I've . . . uh . . . played a few games with Chad. It's a good game."

"It's a *white* man's game," B. J. declared.

"That's what they used to say about golf until Tiger Woods came along," Kirk reminded his friend. "Come on. Lighten up. Chess is just a game. Anybody can play it—you don't have to be white."

B. J. looked at Kirk and shook his head. "You know what, Howie?" he said. "You're getting weirder all the time."

B. J. grabbed Kirk's arm and pretended to rub the blackness off. "I'm thinking maybe you're a white guy who painted himself black because black guys have more fun," he said.

Kirk laughed. "Hey, we've been together since we were kids," he said. "If I were white, you'd know it by now."

"Well, if you're not too busy playing *chess* with *Chad*, maybe you'd like to shoot some baskets with me and Tuck after school," B. J. said.

"You're on," Kirk said. "If I can't cut it in college, maybe I'll become a Harlem Globetrotter."

B. J. rolled his eyes. "You still holding on to that fantasy about going to college?" he asked. "Your old man's a clerk in a grocery store, and your mom's in a wheelchair. Where do you think the money for college is going to come from, the tooth fairy?"

Kirk shrugged. "I'm saving as much as I can from my job," he said. "And Mr. Ha says he always keeps his eyes open for scholarships for his students . . ."

"Yeah, right," B. J. said. "Guys like you and me get scholarships real easy. How does Ha think we can compete against all those other kids applying for those scholarships?"

"Like Mr. Ha says, we just have to put forth more effort . . ." Kirk offered. He knew his argument sounded weak.

" 'Like Mr. Ha says,' " B. J. mimicked. "You'd better watch it or everyone's going to start calling you teacher's pet. You hear what I'm saying?"

Kirk resented B. J.'s remark. "I'm not his pet," he said. "But Mr. Ha's a smart guy with an education. He knows what it takes to make it in the world."

"Oh, right, like teaching in this dump is making it in the world," B. J. laughed. He shook his head. "You are one crazy dude, Howie," he said. "I'm going to P.E. now. At least that's one class I'm doing all right in."

Kirk sighed as he watched his friend walk away. Maybe B. J. and Tucker were right. Maybe making it meant doing what you wanted to do—even if it was dropping out of school. But for Kirk, it meant becoming an engineer. And he didn't want to have to settle for less if he could help it.

He turned then and headed for English. He didn't much like that class. They wrote a lot of papers, and writing was something that didn't come easily to Kirk. Right now he had a B minus in the class. He had always struggled to get his thoughts down on paper. But he knew he'd have to write essays for any scholarships he applied for. So he worked hard to improve his skills.

Kirk had always had to work hard in school. Luckily, he had a mother who thought education was important—and she never let him forget it.

"Honey," his mother had once told him, "someday you'll be wearing a hard hat and walking around some big, important construction site. But you won't be the fellow moving the dirt around. No, sir. You'll be the one who planned the project—the engineer who tells the foremen what to do."

Kirk had grinned at his mother. Even though she had to use crutches or a wheelchair to get around, she had more spirit than any of the mothers of his friends. Several years earlier, she had been diagnosed with multiple sclerosis and now lived with chronic pain. But on top of being a wife and a mother, she worked part-time as a teacher's aide. She helped kids with disabilities so that they could be taught in the regular classrooms.

But sometimes Kirk became discouraged at school. Especially when he got a bad grade on a test he'd studied really hard for. Then he would be tempted to join his friends and not take school seriously.

"A lot of good studying did you," Tucker would point out. "You might just as well give up all that book stuff, Howie. Just hang out and have fun—like the rest of us. Life is too short to waste it working so hard."

But then Kirk would think of his mother. She refused to let a serious disease get in her way. So Kirk couldn't let the arduous work or his friends' remarks steer him off the course he was headed for. But it was hard.

Garrison High was about 30 percent black and 10 percent Hispanic, with a sprinkling of Asian, Middle Eastern, and Eastern European kids. The rest of the kids were white. But even though the student population had become more diverse over the years, Kirk noticed that most kids hung out with their own kind. Like the kids from Bosnia were almost always together in a little group. So were the students from Iraq or Vietnam.

When kids went to the cafeteria at lunchtime, they'd look for others like themselves to sit with. For the most part,

Kirk did too. But sometimes Chad or other members of the chess club would invite him to sit with them. And whenever he did, all the black kids would be on his case for "going white."

"Hey, Howie, you're forgetting who you are!" someone was sure to say.

"Aren't we good enough for you?" another would ask. "Maybe you don't like rap anymore. Maybe you'd rather listen to *opera* music."

It was as if a line were drawn around you and all the kids like you. And no one was supposed to cross that line.

But Kirk knew that if he became an engineer someday, he'd *have* to cross that line. His friends were right. There weren't as many black professionals as there should be. So when a person like Kirk entered a profession, chances were good that he'd be dealing mostly with non-blacks. Kirk figured that if that was the case, he might as well learn to get along with them now.

2 As he had promised, Kirk met Tucker and B. J. after school to shoot baskets. Tucker was in unusually high spirits as he came off the street into the school yard. He was flashing a wad of bills too.

"Hey, man," B. J. laughed, "where'd you get all those pictures of old, dead presidents?"

Tucker chuckled. "I'm just a man doing a man's work," he said, taking the ball from B. J. "If you two weren't so busy playing school, I'd cut you in on my operation."

"Did you drop out of the Reps and get yourself a job?" B. J. joked.

Tucker laughed heartily. "Jobs are for chumps," he said. He dribbled the ball and tossed it into the basket with an easy one-handed motion. "My life has become a slam dunk, homies. While you're sweating over some pin-the-tail-on-the-donkey test, I'm raking in the prime cash!"

Kirk grabbed the rebound and shot from the arch. Without touching the rim, the ball slipped silently through the net. "Now you've got *me* curious," he said.

"Where'd you get the money, Tuck? Did you mug somebody or something?"

Tucker laughed again but didn't offer any information. "Just keep shooting the ball, my man," he said.

For the next hour, the trio played hard. All three were good ball handlers and excellent shots. And even though the game was only for fun, each played as if he were going for a championship.

When dusk started to settle, Tucker consulted the gold watch he wore on his wrist. "Hey, I've got to go. I'm pretty busy these days. When the sun goes down, business goes up. Now you brothers hurry on home and do your homework. And you be sure to tell your mamas to pack you a good lunch tomorrow, 'cause you are growing *boys*!" He laughed as he headed toward his Honda Prelude.

When Tucker was gone, B. J. turned to Kirk and said, "He's right. I'm almost 18 years old. I keep asking myself what I'm doing sitting in classrooms listening to teachers talk about stuff I don't even care about. Did you hear what Tuck said? He's got a *life*, man. He's cruising while we're stalled!"

Kirk opened his mouth to speak but closed it again. What he wanted to say would just prove to B. J. once more that he was "going white." So he just picked up the ball and sank another perfectly executed three-pointer.

* * *

When Kirk got home, he showed his algebra test to his mother. Leona Howell was sitting at the kitchen table, slicing vegetables for a casserole.

"Oh, Kirk!" she cried. "This is wonderful! I know that Mr. Ha is one of the hardest teachers at Garrison. I am so proud of you! Kandy, come and see the high grade your brother got on his algebra test!"

Kandace came from the living room where she'd been dusting for her mother. "A 98! Wow, that's pretty good, Kirk," she said.

"Kirk's going to be the first one in our family to go to college," Mrs. Howell said proudly. "And *you're* going to be the second, Kandace."

Just then Mr. Howell walked in. He'd just gotten off work at the grocery store.

"Pete," Mrs. Howell said, "Kirk got a 98 on his algebra test!"

Kirk's dad tossed his jacket over a chair and smiled at his son. "Nice going, kid. You've got a good head on your shoulders. I aced math, too, when I was your age."

"Thanks, Pop," Kirk said.

"It's on to college for this boy, that's for sure," Mrs. Howell said.

"I've got to check the fluids in the car before it gets dark. How about lending me a hand, Kirk?" his father asked.

"Sure," Kirk replied, following his father out to the garage.

The Howells owned a single-story home in a lower middle class neighborhood. They maintained their house and yard nicely. But many of the neighboring houses were rental properties, and it was obvious that there was no pride of ownership. Many lawns sported huge brown spots, and a few yards had wildly overgrown shrubs. The people across the street had even put two junk cars up on blocks in their front lawn. It bothered Kirk every time he looked at it.

"Your mother and I are really glad you're doing so well in school, Kirk,"

Mr. Howell said, opening up the hood of the older-model station wagon.

"Thanks, Pop," Kirk replied. But he noticed a cautionary tone to his father's voice.

"But sometimes your mother is a bit . . . unrealistic," Mr. Howell went on.

"What do you mean?" Kirk asked.

"Well, she has very high hopes for you," his dad replied. "And that's all right—as long as they're within reason."

"Within reason?" Kirk repeated. "What are you getting at, Pop?" He handed his father a rag to wipe off the oil dipstick.

"I just don't want you to get your hopes up so high that you end up disappointed," Mr. Howell went on. "You're old enough to know what the score is. You should know that you can't believe all that stuff about becoming anything you want. Those people who tell you that it doesn't matter what color you are or if your folks are rich or poor are wrong. Just plain wrong. You have to understand that the playing field isn't level, Kirk. It never has been, and it never will be."

Kirk sighed. This is not what I need to hear, he thought. I get enough downers from Tucker and B. J. I don't need them from my father too.

"You can scramble up that ladder as fast as you want, Kirk. But there's always a chance—a good chance—that at the top there's a big foot just waiting to kick you back down. And there's nothing you can do about it," his father said, examining the dipstick. "It's about a quart low. Hand me one of the cans of oil, will you?"

"But I'm willing to work really hard, Pop," Kirk said, taking a can off the shelf. "I plan on becoming an engineer."

"You're going to *try* to become an engineer," Mr. Howell pointed out as he opened the can and began pouring oil into the oil fill. "And I applaud you for that. But when you get your diploma and go for that first job interview, there will probably be some white guys there deciding if they want you around. Maybe they will. And maybe they won't."

He removed the radiator cap then and checked the water level. "Looks good," he announced. He replaced the cap and slammed the hood closed. Then he turned and laid his hand on Kirk's shoulder. "Just don't let your mother's Pollyanna ideas fool you into thinking it's a walk in the park out there," he advised.

"I won't, Pop," Kirk promised. He understood where his father was coming from. Mr. Howell had been passed over for promotions at work more than once. Kirk knew his dad thought it was because he was black. And maybe he was right. But things would be different with Kirk's generation. Kids were taught to be more tolerant now. True, most kids at school hung out with their own kind, but Kirk and Chad got along fine together. They had a lot in common between their love for math and their determination to become engineers. Kirk could easily imagine an engineering firm where he and Chad and a lot of guys like them worked together.

He could imagine it, and he hoped it was so.

* * *

Every Saturday night, Kirk, B. J., and Tucker cruised down Central Avenue, taking in the street scene. Kirk knew that Tucker spent almost every other evening with the Reps. But Tuck reserved Saturday nights for Kirk and B. J.

Kirk liked being with his old friends, though lately they'd begun to do a few things that scared him. Like loading up on beer every weekend. Tucker had gotten drunk the week before, and Kirk had had to take the wheel for the drive home.

Now Tucker drove, bobbing his head to the rap music booming from his radio. They'd been cruising for a couple of hours, meeting people they knew, and stopping now and then to talk.

Tucker turned on to Twelfth Avenue, one of the roughest streets in the neighborhood. Twelfth Avenue was a kind of dividing line between the different gang turfs in the area. As a result, gangs often tangled there, challenging one another for control of the street. Now the Raiders lounged smugly around a pay phone in front of a deli. The Raiders often tangled with the Red Princes.

"Look at those stiff dudes," Tucker said. "They think they're ice, but they're cowards. The Raiders busted up a party my cousin was having last month. They trashed the place."

"Keep moving, Tuck," Kirk said. "I don't like the looks of those guys."

B. J. laughed. "When did you get to be such a chicken, Howie? Must be from hanging out with that chess-playing white dude at school."

"I'm not a chicken," Kirk replied. "I just want to live to see my eighteenth birthday, that's all. Those guys might be cowards. But they'll still kill you if they don't like you."

But rather than driving on, Tucker cruised to the curb opposite the guys at the pay phone. The Raiders turned then and stared at the three boys in the Prelude.

Kirk knew the routine. You stared back if somebody stared at you, just to prove how tough you were. But sometimes somebody pulled a gun, and there was shooting.

Now Kirk saw one of the gang members reach inside his jacket and pull out something shiny. It looked like a weapon.

"What are you doing, Tuck?" he cried. "Floor it!"

Tucker sped from the curb and roared down the street. "What's the matter with you, Howie?" he demanded.

"I think that tall, skinny guy in the stocking cap was reaching for a gun or something," Kirk said. "I saw him pulling something shiny out of his jacket."

"Are you sure?" B. J. asked.

"Yeah, I'm sure. Look, you guys, I don't want any part of this stuff. Let's just go get something to eat!" Kirk said.

"Those Raiders are getting big ideas," Tucker said. "They act like they own the hood. Well, I'm here to tell them that they don't. It's time we cut them down to size."

"Who's 'we'?" Kirk wanted to know.

"Us—the Reps," Tucker said. "Our guys."

"You mean *your* guys," Kirk corrected him. "I don't want any part of being in a gang."

"Hey, man, chill," Tucker said. "It's nothing but friends being tight, looking out for one another. Nobody messes with the Reps or their girls. Like my girl, Rayna. Some dudes from Twelfth Avenue hassled her when she was walking home from the store. So me and some Reps went over there and showed them some muscle. They backed right off, I'm telling you."

"Howie," Tucker went on, "you remember in middle school when some bullies started hassling you? Who stood up for you, man? It was me and B. J. and the rest of the guys—Roell, Desmond, and Mike. Or don't you remember anything about that anymore?"

Kirk was over six feet tall now. But back in eighth grade he had looked more like a sixth-grader. Some of the bigger guys gave him trouble then. Some days, they'd knock his lunch tray from his hands. Other times, they would jam him against the lockers, demanding money from him. Tucker, B. J., and the others had come to Kirk's rescue more than once, proving there was strength in numbers. Kirk would *never* forget that.

"Sure, I remember what you guys did for me," Kirk admitted. "But it's different now. We're not up against bullies. Nobody bothers us at Garrison—"

"Nobody bothers *you*, you mean," B. J. cut in. "But what about the other brothers and sisters? What about my lady, Loreena, heading to class the other day? Some guys from the hood followed her down the hall, talking trash to her the whole way. Some of us get bothered plenty."

They pulled into a hamburger joint and ordered from the drive-through. Then they sat in the car eating. Kirk had ordered a cola. But Tucker and B. J. were both drinking beer from a cooler they kept behind the driver's seat.

"I don't think you guys ought to be drinking," Kirk remarked.

"What is *with* you tonight, Howie?" Tucker complained. "You're acting like a little old gray-haired granny."

"Look, I just don't want any trouble, okay?" Kirk said.

"Don't worry. We're cool," Tucker said. He popped a french fry into his mouth and glanced out the window. "Man, the night is alive with excitement. Can you feel it? Tate is partying right now at his apartment. He's got a lot of girls coming over. What do you say we head over there when we're done?"

Tate was Tucker's older brother.

"No thanks," Kirk said. "If you guys are going over there, you can take me home. I probably should get going anyway."

"Man, you are getting to be one stick-in-the-mud," B. J. said.

Tucker winked at B. J. "I've got a way to liven him up," he said.

B. J. smiled knowingly as Tucker reached under the seat and pulled out a bottle. He removed the cap and took a long drink. Then he passed the bottle to B. J.

"Is that *whiskey*?" Kirk cried. "You guys are crazy drinking that. It's bad enough that you're sitting in a public parking lot drinking beer. But whiskey! Man, you could get us in so much trouble."

Tucker laughed. "Haven't you ever had whiskey, Howie? You're almost 18 years old."

"I've had it, but I didn't like it," Kirk said. "It made me gag."

"You need to have some of *this* whiskey, man," B. J. said, wiping his mouth with the back of his hand. He offered the bottle to Kirk. "This is some *smooth* stuff."

Kirk shook his head. "I don't think so," he said.

B. J. and Tucker looked at each other. "Man, what are we going to do with this boy?" Tucker asked.

"Yeah, you're going soft on us, Howie," B. J. said.

"Soft? I'm not going soft," Kirk protested.

"Well, then what *do* you call it?" Tucker demanded. "You don't want to do anything we want to do anymore. You're nagging us all the time like you're our old lady or something. I thought we were *friends*, man. Friends don't treat friends like you've been treating us."

"Yeah, next thing you know, you won't even want to go cruising with us on Saturday nights," B. J. said.

Kirk felt guilty then. He knew that Tucker and B. J. were right. He had changed, but they hadn't. And he had no right to criticize them as much as he did.

He stared at the bottle then. So what was the big deal in taking a swallow of whiskey? he wondered. He didn't want his friends to think he was a total wimp. "Okay, all right, give me that bottle," Kirk said.

"Now you're talking," B. J. said, smiling.

Kirk put the bottle to his lips and took a sip of the amber liquid. "Tastes awful," he shuddered.

"You don't drink it for the taste, fool," Tucker said, laughing. "You drink it so the top of your head rises up a little and your feet don't hit the ground when you walk. You hear what I'm saying?"

"Yeah, take another drink. A big one," B. J. urged.

Kirk tipped the bottle and took a long drink. "There," he said, grimacing as he handed the whiskey to B. J. "Are you satisfied?"

"One more," B. J. said. "One more, and you'll know what Tuck was talking about."

But Kirk pushed the bottle away. "That's enough," he said. He was already starting to feel a little giddy.

"Aw, look at the baby boy here," B. J. teased. "What's the matter? Doesn't your mama allow you to drink whiskey? Your mama just wants her little college boy to drink milk and orange juice . . ."

"You've got to learn how to handle your drink, cuz," Tucker told Kirk. "Otherwise you'll never be a *man*."

Kirk sighed. He knew it was stupid to let his friends bulldoze him into doing things he didn't want to do. But their needling was getting to him. He grabbed the bottle and took another long drink. "*Now* are you satisfied? Now, take me home," he demanded.

Tucker shrugged. "Whatever you say, man."

By the time they reached the Howells' house, Kirk was feeling queasy. He fumbled his way out of the car and staggered up the sidewalk. All the way to the door, he could hear Tucker and B. J. laughing.

"Look at the brother," B. J. roared. "He can't even walk straight. He's not used to drinking like a man!"

"Hey, Howie!" Tucker shouted. "Your mama's going to be mad at you. She might send you to bed without your milk and cookies."

But Kirk didn't turn around and answer. It was taking all the concentration he could muster just to reach the front door.

3 At school on Monday, Kirk got an unpleasant shock in P.E. class. The guy from Twelfth Avenue was there. And now he was staring at Kirk from across the gym. The kid didn't have his stocking cap on, but Kirk was sure it was him. He wondered if the guy had seen him clearly in the car and recognized him too. From the hostile glare on his face, it seemed likely.

A few minutes later, the kid approached Kirk. "You're a Rep, huh?" he growled softly.

"I'm nothing," Kirk snapped back. "I don't know what you're talking about. I'm a Falcon. I play on the basketball team. You got a problem with that?"

"Don't get mouthy with me, little man," the boy hissed. "I know what you are."

"Come on, you guys," Coach Bromley shouted. "Let's get some good, healthy exercise going. You're not here to stand around and shoot the breeze. Start out with three laps around the gym."

Kirk realized that he must have seen the guy in P.E. before. But he had never paid any attention to him. There were about 50 kids in Kirk's P.E. class, and Kirk didn't know all of them.

Now, as he ran laps, Kirk was on edge. Every time the Raider took a corner, he glared back at Kirk. Kirk pretended not to notice. If he refused to play the staring game, maybe the kid would realize that Kirk wasn't a Rep.

But later, as Kirk headed for algebra, the kid stepped into his path. "Hey, Rep, you think you're big stuff, don't you?" he sneered.

"I told you I don't know what you're talking about," Kirk said. "I don't know you, and you don't know me. Let's leave it at that, huh?"

"I saw you the other night, man," the kid seethed. "You were riding with Tucker Chandler. You were giving me and the other brothers the stare. Chandler's a Rep. And you wouldn't be with him if you weren't one too. My name's Bones. And you'll be hearing from me, cuz." With that he strolled away.

Kirk had a hard time concentrating on algebra. He felt like the walls were closing in around him. He didn't want any part of the Red Princes. But his friends belonged, so what was he supposed to do? Dump his buddies? His thoughts were interrupted by Mr. Ha's soft voice.

"Now then," Mr. Ha said, "I have written a problem on the board. We want to simplify the equation. Who will volunteer?"

No hands went up.

"Kirk?" Mr. Ha said.

Kirk struggled to concentrate on the equation on the chalkboard. "Um . . . you . . . um . . . make both sides larger by the same number," he replied.

Kirk heard an echoing whine behind him.

"Ooooo . . . you make both sides larger by the same number," B. J. whispered.

"My goodness, but isn't that boy clever?" Desmond said.

"He's so clever he doesn't have to take off his shoes when he counts," B. J. laughed.

"Boys," Mr. Ha said, "if you can't contribute to the lesson, please keep your comments to yourselves."

But the remarks didn't stop. Mr. Ha was a good teacher, but he wasn't a firm disciplinarian. It was not in his nature to be iron-fisted. His class periods were often disrupted by the less serious students, making it difficult for the serious students to learn.

Out in the hallway after class, Chad said to Kirk, "Do you believe the clowns in this class? They're clueless in algebra, so they're determined to make it harder for everybody else. I'm so sick of them disrupting class every day. Don't you wish they'd just drop out?"

Kirk didn't know what to say. Sometimes he felt the way Chad did. But B. J. was a friend. And he was barely hanging on in school by his fingernails. There was still hope for him, if only slim hope. Kirk didn't want B. J. to join the ranks of dropouts who would never have any chance for a good life. And Kirk knew that if B. J. quit school, the Red Princes would swallow him whole. Then he would never be anything but a gang member— and maybe even a dead gang member at that.

B. J. was just heading out the door with Roell and Desmond. He overheard Chad's comment. "You got a problem with us, Spencer?" he demanded.

"Yeah," Chad shot back. "I got a problem with you guys making rude remarks all during class. You bother people who want to learn something. What are you doing here if you aren't interested in learning?"

"Drop dead, man," B. J. said.

Chad laughed and shook his head. "Kirk, these guys are hopeless. Do you want to go to the library with me and study—in peace and quiet?"

Kirk glanced at B. J., who was staring at him, obviously wondering what he was going to do. Was Kirk going to trot off to the library with Chad and prove to his old friend that he really was "turning white" on him?

"Uh, thanks anyway, Chad. But I'll get the books I need later," Kirk said. He moved over to where B. J., Roell, and Desmond stood.

"Suit yourself," Chad said, walking away.

"What's the matter, Kirk, you ashamed to hang with the white dude in front of us?" B. J. taunted.

"B. J., what do you want to make trouble for?" Kirk asked.

"You're a regular little teacher's toady, aren't you?" B. J. growled. "I remember in middle school when you'd get in trouble with the teachers just like we did. But no more. You're so white now you make snow look dark!"

"Hey, give me a break," Kirk argued. "My parents want me to make good grades, okay?"

Kirk was trying to shift the blame for his diligence to his parents. He thought blaming them would take the heat off himself. But he wished he had the courage to come right out and tell B. J. and all the guys the truth. That he really loved math, and he wanted to do well in it so that he could become an engineer.

Kirk yearned to look B. J. right in the eye and shout, "I'm an A student in math because I work hard! And I'm going to college and make something of myself—because that's what I want to do! Deal with it!"

But Kirk didn't have the courage to do that. It would be like telling B. J. and

Tucker and the rest of the guys that their accusations were true. That he had moved beyond them, above them. That they weren't in his league anymore. It would be a slap in the face to the guys Kirk really cared about. And Kirk couldn't do that. Not now. Maybe not ever.

"Hey, I've got to get to class," Kirk said. "I'll talk to you guys later."

As he walked away, he could hear the three of them grumbling among themselves. He was sure they were talking about him.

After school, Kirk worked at the hot dog stand, dishing out corn dogs and sauerkraut dogs and hot mustard dogs. Deana Magee and her sister, Tania, came up to his stand as he was ready to leave. Kirk and Deana had been dating since the beginning of the semester.

"Are you coming to my cousin Bo's birthday party, Kirk?" Deana asked. "It's Sunday night, you know, at the rec center."

"I plan on it," Kirk said.

"Bo is going to be 16 on Sunday," Deana continued. "We're having a deejay and everything."

Kirk smiled at Deana. She was a pretty girl with sparkling brown eyes. She was smart too. Luckily, her best subject was English, Kirk's weakest area. So she could help him when he needed it.

"We're inviting almost everybody," Tania said. "So it should be a lot of fun."

"Everybody—like Tucker and B. J.? And Roell and Desmond?" Kirk wanted to know. He wasn't sure what prompted him to ask. It's just that those guys had always been part of the neighborhood kids who went to the same parties.

The smile left Deana's face. "We invited B. J. and Roell and Desmond. But Bo didn't want Tucker there. You know the kind of stuff Tucker's into now. I don't think Bo wants a Rep swaggering in and making trouble."

"But, Deana," Kirk said softly, "Tucker's a good friend of mine. He's always been included in stuff . . ."

"Kirk, get real, okay?" Deana said. "This isn't going to be a gang party. We just want regular kids. Bo doesn't want any funerals the day after his sixteenth birthday party!"

"Has anybody told Tucker he's not invited?" Kirk asked.

"No, we just didn't invite him," Tania said. "He'll figure it out. He's not stupid."

"Well, then the other three probably won't come if Tucker isn't invited," Kirk said.

"That's their choice," Deana snapped. Immediately, she softened her voice and added, "I'm sorry. I didn't mean to sound so sharp. It's just that this is supposed to be a *birthday* party, Kirk. We don't want any trouble. Remember that graduation party two years ago? It turned out to be like a war with the two gangs shooting it out. Jenna Baker was shot, and now she can't walk. You think Bo wants something like that to happen at *his* party?"

"I guess not," Kirk said. But he still wished *everybody* included Tucker.

* * *

The next day in algebra class, Kirk overheard Roell and B. J. talking.

"Are you going to Bo's party, man?" Roell asked.

"Yeah, I guess so," B. J. replied.

"Tucker's not invited," Roell said. "You know that, don't you?"

B. J.'s eyes grew wide. "No way! Are you telling me the truth, man?"

"Yeah," Roell said. "I guess the Magees are getting real white. They've got no use for their old friends."

"Then I'm not going to that party, either," B. J. declared. "If Tucker's not welcome, they can do without me too."

"That's exactly the way I feel," Roell agreed.

Kirk felt miserable. Just as he had feared, if Tucker wasn't invited, the others wouldn't come. He made up his mind to talk to Bo Magee about it. Maybe he could convince Bo to let Tucker come.

After school, Kirk found Bo Magee where he thought he would. In the gym, shooting baskets. Bo was a good basketball player who practiced year-round.

"Hey, Bo," Kirk called as he walked across the gym. "I hear you're having quite a birthday bash on Sunday."

Bo grinned. "Yeah, the place is going to be hopping," he said. "Lots of girls there and all kinds of great music."

"Well, could I ask you a favor?" Kirk said when he reached the other boy.

"Shoot," Bo replied, sinking a basket from the free throw line.

"Tucker Chandler is a good friend of mine. Do you think there's any chance you could let him come to the party?" Kirk asked.

Bo retrieved the ball then and turned to face Kirk. "Tucker Chandler's bad news," he said. "I don't think I want him there."

"He's had some bad breaks, Bo, but he's basically a good guy," Kirk said. "Remember when we'd all shoot baskets together? Tuck taught you a lot of good moves."

Bo looked thoughtful for a moment. "Yeah, Kirk, I remember," he said. "Those were some good times. But now he's driving a fancy car, and he's got enough money to buy silk suits. The rap on the street is that he's dealing. Maybe crack."

"I don't think he's dealing, Bo," Kirk said. "But I think he might be right on the edge. I think he could go either way. That's why his friends are so important now. We're his connection to better days.

If we all just cut him loose, then he's gone.

"You remember when B. J.'s mother died and he was close to doing something desperate?" Kirk went on. "Remember how we hung with him till he put himself back together? We've always been there for one other in this neighborhood. Even in really bad times. I think we might be able to pull Tucker back from the edge if we try."

Bo thought for another moment. "I don't know. I don't want any trouble at this party," he said. "A guy only turns 16 once in his life. I want the memories of this party to be good ones, not bad ones."

"He'll be fine," Kirk assured Bo. "I'll keep an eye on him. I promise."

"Well, okay," Bo said slowly, "Tucker can come. But he'd better know going in that the rec room where we're having the party is *nobody's* turf. If he happens to see somebody from Twelfth Avenue, he has to be cool. Can you make him understand that, Kirk?"

"You got it," Kirk said, grasping Bo's hand. "Thanks, brother. I won't forget this."

4 The recreation center was rocking with music when Kirk arrived. He grinned to see so many familiar faces. He had to admit that as much as he liked Chad and enjoyed playing chess with him sometimes, nothing could equal the comfortable feeling he got when he was with old friends.

This was where Kirk felt at home. These were his people. It was so easy to be with the people he had known all his life. He shared the same memories. And he laughed at the same jokes and enjoyed the same music as his friends. He shared none of that kind of camaraderie with Chad.

Tucker Chandler was one of the last to show up. He swaggered in with Rayna on his arm. Tucker wore a black silk suit and a gold chain around his neck. Rayna was dressed in a tight midnight blue dress and high heels. Kirk was standing nearby as Tucker placed an elegantly wrapped package on the table with Bo's gifts.

There was a big, hand-lettered card on the package that read, "To Bo Magee, who learned the two-hand chest pass from me. Tuck." Bo looked a little leery when he saw it, and Kirk was relieved when Bo smiled at Tucker.

Kirk approached his old friend and said warmly, "I'm glad you're here, Tuck."

"You're the reason I'm here, Howie," Tucker said. "Don't think I don't know that. Tucker Chandler knows everything that goes down in the hood, and you better believe it."

"I don't doubt that," Kirk laughed.

"You still kicking around those old halls of Garrison?" Tucker teased.

"Yeah, I am," Kirk replied. "Looks like I'll be there till the end. How about you? You ever thought about getting your GED?"

Tucker frowned. "Say what?"

"Your GED—general equivalency diploma. You take a test. And if you pass, it's like you've got a high school diploma," Kirk explained.

"Put a lid on that stuff, bro'," Tucker laughed. "I don't need a GED! I told you, my man, school is kids' stuff. I'm all done with that. I'm cruising Main Street now, and I don't need any training wheels on my bike. Understand? I got business connections right now, Kirk. I'm on my way."

"Tucker, whatever you're doing, it's probably going to jump up and bite you eventually," Kirk warned. "There's no easy way to make it in life. Like my dad says, easy money turns out to cost more than the other kind. You remember Big Joe Waite? When we were in fifth grade, we all looked up to that big, bad dude like he was the heart of cool. We all thought he was the man. Well, when he got shipped off to do 40 years to life, he didn't look so cool then."

Tucker laughed again, his big, hearty laugh. "You aren't scaring me, boy. Takes more than horror stories about some big, dumb guy from years ago to scare me. I'm smart, Howie. I don't need a diploma. All I need is what I've got—and I've got it good right now."

Tucker put his arm around Rayna's waist and said, "Let's dance, baby."

"You got it," Rayna smiled.

"Speaking of dancing, how about you and me?"

Kirk heard a voice behind him and turned to see Deana standing there. She was wearing a sleek white dress and shimmering earrings.

"You look *great!*" he said.

"You don't look so bad yourself, home boy," Deana said. "You with anybody?"

"Nobody but you," Kirk replied. Smiling, he swept her onto the dance floor.

At 10:00, the dancing paused while Bo opened his gifts. Most of the guys had gotten him CDs. Some of the girls gave him weird T-shirts and baseball caps. Kirk knew Bo loved sports memorabilia, so he had gotten him a framed rookie card of Mike Piazza, one of Bo's favorite baseball players. But Tucker gave Bo a beautiful gold watch that caused a ripple of amazement through the room.

"Hey, man, you didn't steal this, did you, Tuck?" Bo asked, half in humor and half serious.

"Sure," Tucker laughed.

When Bo put on the watch, everybody came over to admire it.

Later, Bo talked to Kirk. "You know, you were right. Tucker is a good guy. I never saw anybody so generous. It's not just because he gave me the watch either.

I heard he gave Leon Baker some money for an operation his kid sister needs. The brother has really got it together."

"Yeah," Kirk agreed, but many fears coursed through his mind. How does a 17-year-old get ahold of enough money to buy such a flamboyant watch? he wondered. And how does he do it in an honest way?

"I remember him at Garrison," Bo said, "with everybody calling him stupid and putting him down. But, man, look at him now. You've got to hand it to the brother. You've really got to."

Kirk looked around the room until he spotted Tucker. He was standing in the midst of a crowd of kids. Kirk noticed that many of them were having the same reaction to Tucker as Bo had. Tucker was dressed well, and he carried himself with the demeanor of a powerful and influential person. He was more like a rap star or a professional basketball player than a neighborhood kid with money.

Even Kirk couldn't help feeling a rush of admiration. Tucker was the center of attention at this party, while Kirk just blended into the background. Tucker seemed to have all the money he needed and plenty of time to spend it. Kirk was struggling to finish high school. Then he'd be beating his brains out for another five or six years to get an engineering degree. And then, who really knew what waited for him out there? Tucker seemed to be getting it all, and he was getting it with almost no effort.

"Look at the man," Kirk said enviously to Deana. "He's got it made. No sweat. No worry. He's like that Midas guy in that myth. Everything is turning to gold in his hands."

Deana shrugged and said, "I think something smells fishy, Kirk. We have plenty of guys like that in the hood. We've always had the cool cats. That's what my dad called them when he was our age. The cool cats. They wore sports jackets, and they had wads of money a couple inches thick. They were warlords in the gangs, and the rich ones dealt dope to the junkies. Dirty money."

"I don't think Tucker does that," Kirk said.

"You don't know that for sure," Deana pointed out.

"No, that's right, I don't," Kirk said. "But Tuck's my friend. We've been real close since we were little kids. I think I'd know if he was dealing."

On the way home that night, Kirk thought about Tucker, envying him, then being apprehensive for him. If he wasn't dealing drugs, what could he possibly be doing to make so much money?

* * *

"How was the party last night?" Kandace asked at the breakfast table Monday morning.

"Great," Kirk said, loading his plate with scrambled eggs and sausage.

"See, Mom?" Kandace said. "It was a nice party. You should have let me go."

"You're 12 years old, sweetie," Mrs. Howell said. "Kirk, were there any 12-year-olds at the party?"

"I didn't see any," Kirk said with a smile at his sister.

As usual, Kirk's father ate his breakfast

silently while reading the morning paper. But when Kirk mentioned Tucker Chandler, his dad looked up from his reading. "How's that boy doing? Last I heard he was finally out of the foster care system. That kid has had a rough life."

"He's doing really well, Pop," Kirk said. "He's got his own place, and he drives a nice car."

"Where's he working now? He can't be more than, what, 17? What kind of job do they give to a 17-year-old dropout?" Mr. Howell asked.

"I don't know for sure," Kirk said, not looking up as he put a forkful of eggs into his mouth.

Kirk's father frowned. "He was one of your closest friends," he said. "Why don't you know? Don't you fellows talk?"

Kirk took a swallow of orange juice. "He's doing a little bit of everything, I guess . . . whatever he can find . . ." Kirk said.

"What does *that* mean?" Mr. Howell demanded.

"Well, he's in with the Red Princes now . . . that's a gang," Kirk said.

"I *know* what that is," Mr. Howell barked. "I wasn't born yesterday, you know. There were gangs here when I was a kid. I'd see them doing their rumble strut, flashing their money around. I guess I should have expected it from Tucker. Now you listen to me, Kirk. I don't want you hanging around *anybody* who's in a gang, do you hear? Tucker Chandler or anyone else."

"I think he might get out of the gang, Pop," Kirk said nervously, thinking himself a fool for even mentioning Tucker's affiliation with the Red Princes. Why did he have to blurt that out? "He was really sort of different last night. We were even talking about . . . um . . . him getting his GED."

"Well, just don't get mixed up with gang members, Kirk," his dad warned. "That's a one-way ticket to an early grave."

"Kirk, can I have a ride to school this morning?" Kandace asked. "I want to get there early to work on my science project."

Kirk was grateful for the interruption. "If you're ready in 10 minutes," he said.

"That's when I'm leaving."

When Kirk got to school, he went straight to the computer lab. Normally he had basketball practice before school. But Coach Bromley was attending some training sessions for coaches that week, so Kirk had the morning free. He wanted to finish his research for the paper Ms. Hogan had assigned. All the students had to choose an important 20th-century writer and do a ten-page paper on his or her contribution to literature.

Kirk had chosen Ernest Hemingway. Over the last couple of weeks, he had read three of Hemingway's books and several of his short stories. He'd also found some sources that described how Hemingway's works changed the way fiction was written. All he had left was to search the Internet for background information on Hemingway.

Kirk sat down at an open computer and went to work. Twenty minutes later, he had found what he was looking for. He printed out several pages and then headed for class. He planned on reading the information he'd found that evening and then paraphrasing it for his report, which was due on Friday.

That day, the buzz all around school was about Bo Magee's party. Everyone was talking about what a great party it had been. And in almost every class, Kirk heard the name "Tucker Chandler" thrown about before the first bell rang. Everyone seemed to be really taken by him. Kirk didn't know if that was a good thing or not. He was glad that Tucker was getting some positive attention. But he wondered how many students would be influenced by Tucker's apparent success. How many would drop out, thinking they could have it all as Tucker did? Kirk wondered. And how many new members would the Reps have?

By Wednesday, Kirk had a rough draft of his paper finished. He showed it to his mother, who gave him some pointers on how he might improve it. Then he wrote a final draft. But when he read it over, he saw that it wasn't good enough. He revised it, read it, and then revised it again. Ms. Hogan was a very demanding teacher. And English was Kirk's weakest subject. He wanted this paper to be as perfect as he could make it.

Friday morning, Kirk went to the computer lab for a final time. There he created a cover page and a works cited page for the sources he had used. When he entered Ms. Hogan's classroom later that day, he felt as if his report was as good as he could possibly make it.

Ms. Hogan entered the classroom with the usual somber look on her face. She was a slender, attractive young woman and very dedicated to her teaching. Unlike some of the other teachers who kept ungraded work for a long time, Ms. Hogan returned even the longest assignments to her students quickly. Some of the kids joked that since she was single and so stern she had probably scared all her would-be suitors away, and now she had no social life. So she had plenty of time to grade papers during her lonely evenings at home.

"Pass your papers forward," Ms. Hogan began. "Make sure they're paper-clipped. If you don't have a paper clip, there are some on my desk."

Dutifully, the students passed their reports to the front of the room. Ms. Hogan collected them with this warning. "I trust all the work in these papers is original," she said. "I know that there are lots of papers for sale out there, but I've warned you before about plagiarism. Believe me, if I suspect that your work isn't original, I have my ways of finding out. If anyone has turned in a 'purchased' paper, he or she will be given an F for the quarter, no exceptions."

Kirk saw a few students shift nervously in their seats. He hoped for their sakes that they had written their own papers. He had heard that Ms. Hogan could be ruthless.

5 All weekend, Kirk looked forward to Monday. He thought he'd done a good job on his paper and wanted to find out his grade. He wasn't counting on an A, but he thought a B or B plus would be nice.

But on Monday, Ms. Hogan appeared in the classroom looking more angry than serious. She returned most of the reports. But she withheld four and asked to see those students, one by one, after class.

Kirk was stunned when he realized that his report was among those that had not been returned.

All during class, Kirk agonized over what might be going on. He had worked so hard on his paper. What fault could the teacher possibly have found with it?

After class, Ms. Hogan asked each of the four students in turn to come into her office. The first was Jill Means. She was a pretty good student, but Kirk knew she worried a lot about her grades. He had seen her cheating more than once.

Kirk and the other two students waited nervously while Ms. Hogan met with Jill.

"What do you think this is about?" Kirk asked Letoya Armstrong, who sat beside him. Letoya was close to tears.

"I don't know," she said, wringing her hands. But something about the way she said it made Kirk think that she *did* know.

"She figured us out," Karl Frasier said. He was sitting across from Kirk and Letoya at the table outside Ms. Hogan's office.

"What do you mean she 'figured us out'?" Kirk wanted to know.

Karl shrugged. "She figured out we bought our papers somewhere. Hey, where'd you get yours, Howell? Off the Internet? How much did you have to pay?"

Kirk was astounded at Karl's words. "What are you talking about?" he demanded. But before he could go on, Jill emerged from Ms. Hogan's office. Tears were running down her cheeks.

"She thinks I bought my report!" Jill cried.

"Why would she think that?" Kirk asked.

"She says it's a lot better than anything I've done before," Jill replied, sniffling and taking out a tissue. Then she looked at Kirk and said, "You're supposed to go in next."

Kirk turned numb. He walked stiffly into Ms. Hogan's office and sat down. Ms. Hogan peered at him over her small, fashionable glasses. Though black, Ms. Hogan was so light-skinned that she could have been, and often was, mistaken for white. She wasn't popular with the black students because she seemed to make it a point to disassociate herself from black culture.

"Please have a seat," Ms. Hogan said.

Kirk sat down in a chair next to her desk. His throat was dry, and he could feel his underarms becoming sticky with sweat.

"Kirk, this report you turned in is very good," Ms. Hogan began. "In fact, it is of the quality I would expect from an English major in college."

Kirk wasn't sure how to reply. Was she complimenting him or accusing him?

"And therein lies the problem," the teacher went on.

"What do you mean?" Kirk asked cautiously.

"I mean that, in my opinion, it's unlikely that you wrote this paper," Ms. Hogan said, holding the paper up for Kirk to see.

"You're a decent student, and you work hard. But I don't think you're capable of this quality of work."

"Ms. Hogan, I wrote every word of that paper myself," Kirk said passionately. "I revised it *three times*!"

"The paper doesn't sound like you, Kirk," the teacher said. "It doesn't sound like your 'voice.' When you've been teaching for 11 years, you learn to recognize each student's voice on paper. You don't write this smoothly. At least you never have before. And that is why I'm questioning whether this paper is original."

"So you're saying I plagiarized it?" Kirk asked. A feeling of dread was rising within him.

"Yes, I think you bought this paper somewhere and are claiming it for your own. Probably off of one of those Internet sites," Ms. Hogan replied.

"That's not true, Ms. Hogan," Kirk cried, his voice rising in anger. "It's not true. I did research—lots of it. Just look at my works cited page. And I struggled with that report and polished every sentence just so it would be good!"

"Calm down, Kirk," Ms. Hogan cautioned. "I'm going to spend the next few days searching the Internet. I expect to find the four reports I have withheld. If that proves to be the case, then you and the others will receive Fs for the quarter. You know the rules." She delivered her grim message with the callous manner of a judge.

"But I wrote that paper!" Kirk protested. "You won't find it on the Internet. I swear it!"

"I told you to control yourself," Ms. Hogan warned again. "If I don't find proof of plagiarism, then you'll receive whatever grade you deserve. You may go now, Kirk. Please send in Letoya Armstrong."

Kirk stood up then and stormed out of the office. He flew by the table with the two other students without saying a word. He felt as if he could kick a hole in the wall or rip down one of the posters in the hall without a moment's regret. Anger fused into hatred within him—blind, disbelieving hatred.

* * *

"You'll never believe what Hogan did to me," Kirk told B. J. during lunch.

"Jill told me," B. J. replied. "She's saying you guys got your papers off the Internet."

"Exactly!" Kirk seethed. "B. J., I sweated over that paper, I swear it! I dragged so many books out of the library I almost broke my back. I revised it over and over to get it just right. And she's got the nerve to call me a cheat—when she doesn't even have any proof!" He kept clasping and unclasping his hands. He still felt like punching his fist through something, smashing something.

"She just looks at the color of your skin, Howie, and she can't believe you wrote such a good paper," B. J. said. The paper he had turned in was so poor he'd gotten a D minus. Ms. Hogan *knew* it was his work.

"But, B. J., she's black too! Hasn't she got any faith in her own people?" Kirk cried.

"She's been acting white ever since she came to Garrison," the other boy replied.

"You know that. She doesn't have anything to do with us black kids. Mrs. Barnes jokes around with us a lot. She even brings donuts to class sometimes, even though it's against the rules. She's great."

"I'm so mad I don't even feel like going to any more classes today," Kirk said.

B. J. shrugged and said, "So cut."

Kirk shook his head. "No, I'd better not," he said. "My parents would kill me."

"They won't know," B. J. said. "Loreena works in the office. She'll fix it for you. Come on, cuz, let's bust out and go cruising. Who needs this school? Maybe we can find Tuck, and he can cut us in on some of his action."

But Kirk realized he wasn't ready to do that. He was almost ready, but not quite. He shook his head and said, "No, I don't think so. I was just letting off steam. I'll see you later."

He trudged to his next class and slumped down in his chair. The teacher kept looking at him expectantly, waiting for him to raise his hand as he usually did. But Kirk couldn't do that today. In his mind, he kept going over what Ms. Hogan had done to him. He was incensed at the injustice of being presumed guilty until proven innocent.

And he was angry that Jill Means was going all over the school telling everybody what had happened. Now all the kids were going to think Kirk was a cheat too.

After school, as Kirk walked toward his car, he glanced over to the teachers' parking lot and saw Ms. Hogan approaching her car. Making an impulsive decision, Kirk sprinted over to the teacher.

"Ms. Hogan, is it okay if I bring my notes on that Hemingway paper tomorrow to show you all the steps I went through, the rough drafts and—" Kirk began.

Ms. Hogan barely looked up as she fumbled with her car keys to unlock her car door. "Kirk, I told you I would get back to you about the paper," she said, her voice edged with irritation. "If I need to see your notes, I'll tell you." She unlocked her door and looked at Kirk. "And I really don't appreciate your running up to me like that and scaring me half to death!"

"Scaring you?" Kirk asked in surprise.

"You know me, Ms. Hogan. I'm your student. What's to be scared about?"

"Well, for a moment all I saw was this large, angry-looking figure running toward me. I almost dropped my car keys," Ms. Hogan said.

Kirk looked at her in astonishment. She was afraid of black kids! he realized then. What she really meant to say was that she saw a large, angry-looking *black* figure running toward her.

"You don't like kids like me, do you, Ms. Hogan?" Kirk asked in a bitter voice.

"I resent that remark," Ms. Hogan snapped. "I feel the same way about *all* my students. I just want them to turn in good, honest work."

"I know where you're coming from, Ms. Hogan," Kirk said. "You don't expect much from guys like me. If we do good work, you're pretty sure we cheated because we're all pretty stupid, right? Isn't that what you think of black kids?"

"That's enough, Kirk," Ms. Hogan commanded. "I'm ending this conversation right now." Without another word, she climbed into her car and drove off.

As Kirk watched her drive away, he realized he was scarcely breathing. He was stunned with bewilderment. Ms. Hogan was scared of him! She was afraid he would do her physical harm. How could she assume that of him? Just because his skin was black? Kirk had never hurt anyone—and he never intended to. It made Kirk sick just to think about it.

Slowly he turned and walked back to his car. There he found B. J. waiting for him.

"Can I have a ride home, man?" B. J. asked. "My car's not working, and Loreena has to make up a test."

"Yeah, sure," Kirk replied, still in a daze. "Get in."

The two boys climbed into the car. But for a minute, Kirk just sat staring straight ahead with his hands on the steering wheel.

"What's wrong, man?" B. J. asked. "You still ticked about what Ms. Hogan did?"

Trembling with anger, Kirk explained what had just happened. "She has me tried and convicted, B. J.," he said miserably. "There's no way she's ever going to believe that I wrote that paper."

"What have I been telling you all along, cuz?" B. J. replied. "We've got no friends in this world but each other. That's why I'm thinking about joining the Reps. Tucker says he'll take care of me. He'll take care of you too, Howie. Hey, how about we go see Tuck right now? We can kick back, relax a little. Just the three of us."

Kirk felt so angry and confused. He thought anything that would get his mind off of what had happened to him that day would be welcome. "You got it," he said. He started the car and drove out of the parking lot.

Kirk and B. J. pulled up before a stucco court where Tucker rented a unit. On the outside the place looked plain, but inside it was luxurious. Tucker had a deep pile rug and lots of leather furniture. He had a big-screen TV and a stereo that made Kirk feel as if he were at the recording studio, standing in the midst of the musicians.

"Ms. Hogan busted Howie for cheating, but he didn't do it," B. J. explained to

Tucker as they settled onto the blue leather couch.

"Doesn't surprise me," Tucker said, passing out colas. "Teachers think we brothers aren't capable of anything."

"Hogan is black though," Kirk said, taking a swallow from his can.

"I know that," Tucker said. "But she passes for white. She's white on the inside. She's ashamed of being black." A thin smile came to Tucker's handsome face. "Know what, Howie? This is just what I've been warning you about. You were starting to act white too. Maybe it's a good thing, you getting messed up by a teacher. Because now you see what I mean. Acting white kills your soul, man. Just look at Ms. Hogan.

"I keep telling you two there's a place for you in the Reps," Tucker went on. "I'm getting pretty high up in the gang—getting a lot of respect from the brothers. I'll make sure you're taken care of."

"Hey, what do you say, Howie?" B. J. said. "After what happened to you today, are you ready?"

Kirk looked at his two friends. Suddenly

he felt closer to them than he had in a long time. He felt as he had when they'd protected him from bullies in middle school. The three boys were really tight then. They were brothers—blood brothers. And they still were. Kirk couldn't deny it.

He smiled and said, "I might be. I just might be."

6   When Kirk got home that day, his father was already off work. He was sitting at the kitchen table filling out some insurance forms. Mrs. Howell's condition required regular medical care. And they were constantly filling out forms to submit to the insurance company.

Mr. Howell looked at Kirk and asked, "Where have you been?"

"Just hanging out with . . . B. J.," Kirk said. He didn't want to mention that he had been with Tucker. "Pop, you're not going to believe the day I had. You know that paper I've been working on for English? Well, Ms. Hogan accused me of downloading it from the Internet. She's calling me a cheat. She could ruin my whole high school record by sticking me with an F that I don't deserve."

"What proof has she got?" Mr. Howell asked.

"None, as far as I'm concerned," Kirk said. "She's checking the Internet this weekend to see if she can find my paper."

"But she won't find it, will she? You

didn't download that paper, right?" his dad asked.

"No, I wrote it myself," Kirk said.

"Then she'll have to admit she was wrong," Mr. Howell said. "But this is just the kind of thing I've been warning you about, Kirk. No matter how well you do, there's always the chance someone's going to come along and kick you down."

"It just makes me so mad that she would do a thing like that, accuse me like that. I tried to reason with her after school, and she treated me like some kind of criminal. Said I scared her. Can you beat that?" Kirk said.

"There are a lot of people who are afraid of young black men," Mr. Howell said.

"But it's not fair—and it's not right!" Kirk cried.

"No, it's not," his father replied. "But that's the way it is, and you're going have to come to terms with it."

"But—" Kirk started to protest.

"There are no buts about it," Mr. Howell went on. "So get your head out of that cloud you and your mother have created, and come back down to earth. Life isn't going to be easy on you, boy. You've had two strikes against you from the get-go—you're black and you're not wealthy. You'll always be black. And chances are, you'll never be wealthy. If you accept that now, you'll have a lot less disappointment to face later." He turned his attention back to the insurance forms.

Kirk went into his bedroom and threw himself onto the bed. His father's words rang in his ears, *You'll always be black. And chances are, you'll never be wealthy.*

What was the point then? Kirk asked himself, punching his pillow with all his might. What good did it do to try so hard if he was going to get kicked down by the first person who felt like kicking him down? What good would it do him to get an engineering degree if no one would hire him because he was black? Then he *would* always be poor.

Kirk thought of Tucker then. He wasn't poor anymore. He had enough money to buy expensive gifts for his friends. And to lend them money too. Tucker had taken the shortcut by dropping out of school and joining the Reps—and he'd saved himself a lot of struggle and frustration.

Kirk clenched his teeth and swore to himself that if this paper issue didn't turn out all right, he was going to drop out of school and join the Reps. No buts about it.

* * *

Kirk had a date with Deana that night, but he didn't really feel like going. He couldn't stop thinking about what had happened. But Deana wanted to see a comedy/action film that had just hit the theaters. So Kirk picked her up, and they headed for the mall. He thought that, if nothing else, the movie might get his mind off his troubles.

"I'm sorry about what happened in English, Kirk," Deana said as they drove. "It was really unfair."

"Yeah. I thought if you were honest and did your own work, you'd be okay and nobody would call you a cheat," Kirk said. His hands gripped the wheel more tightly than usual because of the tension he was feeling.

"I guess you must have done some job on that paper, Kirk. It must have been much better than your usual work, and that made her suspicious," Deana said.

"Are you making excuses for Ms. Hogan, Deana?" Kirk snapped.

"Oh, Kirk, of course not. I'm just trying to figure out what happened," Deana replied. "Ms. Hogan is usually pretty fair."

"Well, I don't want any excuses for her. She had no right to treat me like that," Kirk declared emphatically. "Like I was trash. That's because she thinks I am trash. She's acting white, Deana. You notice that? She thinks she's better than the black kids."

"Kirk, you're letting this make you crazy," Deana pointed out.

Kirk turned sharply and glared at Deana. "It's easy for you to brush it off, Deana. It's not happening to you. Nobody is accusing *you* of being a cheat. Ms. Hogan is nice to you, real nice, and do you know why?"

"Well, English is my best subject . . ." Deana offered.

"Yeah, but there's another reason," Kirk

said. "You're not as dark as I am. You have some white ancestors. You told me so yourself. But I'm black through and through. Ms. Hogan thinks guys who look like me have to be stupid—and dangerous. I'm pulling an A in both math and science, but she doesn't want to think about that. In Hogan's book I'm the criminal type— tall, muscular, and black. She gets scared just looking at me."

"Kirk, I think you're blowing this thing out of proportion," Deana replied. "Besides, it's all going to be straightened out when she doesn't find your paper on the Internet. Why are you working yourself up so much? She'll have to give you the A you deserve."

"She'd better," Kirk said as he pulled into the mall parking lot and turned off the car. "She'd better apologize to me and tell the whole class that she made a big mistake. She's got everyone thinking I'm a big cheat. They're all laughing about it. A lot of them resent me anyway because I make good grades. I'm getting it coming and going, Deana, and I'm about to explode!"

Deana reached out and placed her hand over Kirk's hand. "Try to forget about it for a while, okay?" she said. "Let's just go watch the movie and pretend like today didn't happen." She leaned over and kissed him on the cheek then.

Kirk sighed and tried to smile. "I'm sorry," he said. "This is supposed to be a date, isn't it? You're right. Let's go watch the movie."

But the movie didn't cheer Kirk up. In fact, he hardly cracked a smile all through it. Ordinarily he would have enjoyed the antics of the two street detectives, one black and one white. He would have laughed at their banter and gotten caught up in the suspense as they tried to crack a counterfeit ring. But tonight it got on his nerves. Especially when the black cop did something wrong or was made to look foolish.

"What kind of garbage is this?" Kirk growled at one point. "That brother's making a fool of himself."

"Kirk, lighten up. It's a comedy!" Deana whispered.

"Well, it's stupid," Kirk snapped back.

After the movie, Kirk drove Deana to her house. He was still in a glum mood and was looking forward to getting home and going to bed. He just wanted to escape the events of the day. And he thought the best way to do it was to sleep.

"You know, if you were like this all the time, I wouldn't have anything to do with you," Deana said half-seriously as they pulled up to the curb in front of her house.

Kirk sighed. "I don't think you understand how much I'm hurting, Deana," he said. "I don't think anybody understands except maybe B. J. and Tucker and those guys. It's really hard for black men, Deana. We've got to fight all the time just to get a little respect. That's why the gangs look so good to young black men. At least they offer you some respect . . ."

"Kirk, you're not like those guys," Deana said.

"I'm a lot more like them than you think, Deana," Kirk informed her.

"They're losers, Kirk," Deana replied. "You've got a good mind. Look how you aced algebra. I can't believe how well you understand that stuff. You're going places.

Those guys don't know it yet, but they're going nowhere."

"Maybe it's not about brains, Deana," Kirk said. "Maybe it's about heart. Those guys have hearts. If I was really down and out, they'd stick by me. I know they would. They're like family, like brothers. That's no small thing, Deana. You don't take something like that lightly. You don't walk away from guys like that. You stick by them just like they stick by you."

"Kirk, if I mean anything at all to you, you'd better think twice about joining the Reps," Deana said. "Because the minute you do, I'm out of your life forever."

Kirk sighed but didn't reply. He just sat there filled with the frustrations and disappointments of the day. And this was just another one. Join the Reps, and he'd lose Deana. Why did there always have to be a trade-off? he wondered. Why couldn't life be as easy for him as it was for Chad Spencer? Chad knew where he was going and knew exactly how to get there. And he knew that once he arrived, things would go pretty much the way he had planned. And there were no trade-offs involved. Why did Kirk have to make such difficult choices? Why couldn't he just live the life he wanted to live?

* * *

Monday morning at basketball practice, Coach Bromley kept yelling at Kirk. "You're sloppy, Howell. You're not sharp. What's the matter with you?"

When Kirk missed two easy lay-ups, the coach yelled from the sidelines, "Howell! What's your problem? If you keep performing like this, you won't be starting in the next game. You got that?"

Coach Bromley yelled at all the players. That was his way. Kirk knew that, and he had never minded it before. He just took it in stride. But suddenly, Kirk bitterly resented it. A wave of rage swept through him, and he heard his own voice yelling, "Get off my case, Coach! Just leave me alone, okay?"

The coach pulled Kirk off the court then. "You fix that attitude, Howell, or you're done," he threatened. "You get your act together real fast, boy."

"I'm not your *boy*," Kirk snapped, looking the coach straight in the eyes. "I'm not *anybody's* boy. I've got a name, and it's Kirk Howell. So don't call me *boy* again, do you hear?"

Kirk saw something like fear pass over the older man's face. For a minute the coach was silent. Then finally he mumbled, "All right, get back out on the court now and get to work." Quickly he turned away and walked toward the sidelines again.

"Coach, I—" Kirk called, but Coach Bromley wouldn't look at him. He headed to the other end of the court and began working with some of the other players.

Kirk stood rooted to the hardwood floor for a moment, ambivalent about the coach's reaction. He liked Coach Bromley and felt guilty for the altercation they had just had. But Kirk also couldn't help feeling amazed. Amazed that he could have such an effect on people, such control over their emotions. It had happened with Ms. Hogan and now with the coach. Could he scare people into doing what he wanted? he wondered. If so, this was a power he had never known he'd had. He didn't understand it. And it scared him more than he had scared either Ms. Hogan or the coach.

7 Kirk dreaded going to English class that day. He didn't want to face the other students in the class. And he wasn't sure he could even be civil to Ms. Hogan. He hoped she wouldn't call on him.

As he walked into class, he noticed that many of the students who were involved in conversations stopped talking. It was as if he had caught them gossiping about him. He went to his desk and waited in silence for class to begin.

Ms. Hogan came in a few minutes later and took attendance. Then she asked the four students whose tests had been withheld to see her after class in her office. She looked very grim all during class, and Kirk spent the period in anguish. What if she had found something similar to his paper on the Internet? Would that be enough to deny him his grade? he wondered.

When the bell rang, Kirk gathered his books and headed toward Ms. Hogan's office. As before, he sat at the table just outside the door with Letoya and Karl. Jill Means was already in with the teacher.

"Well, I guess we find out today if we're busted," Karl said.

"Speak for yourself, Frasier," Kirk said. "I'm not going to be busted because I wrote my own paper."

Karl shrugged. "If you say so, man," he said.

Kirk could tell Karl didn't believe him.

"I just hope she didn't find mine," Letoya worried.

"You mean it's on there?" Kirk asked. "You got it from the Internet?"

Letoya nodded. "I had to," she said. "I didn't have any time to write it."

"No time?" Kirk said. "You knew about this paper for as long as everybody else did."

"I know," Letoya admitted. "But I'm just so busy. I work, and I have a boyfriend, and . . ."

But before Kirk and Letoya could continue their conversation, Jill came out of Ms. Hogan's office. She was crying even harder than the last time.

"What happened?" Karl asked.

"She found my paper . . . the one I downloaded," Jill sobbed.

"Oh, man, that's rough," Karl said.

"What am I going to do?" Jill cried. "I need this class to graduate." She picked up her stack of books from the table and drew a shaky breath. Then she said, "Kirk, you're supposed to go in next."

"Okay," Kirk replied. He was so tense as he entered the teacher's office that he could hear his heart pounding in his ears.

"Sit down, Kirk," Ms. Hogan said. She cleared her throat then and began. "Let me begin by saying that I failed to find your paper on the Internet."

Kirk breathed a sigh of relief. It was over! She hadn't found it, and now she would have to admit that she had been wrong.

"But that still doesn't mean that you wrote the paper," the teacher added.

"What do you mean?" Kirk asked in disbelief.

"There are many ways to obtain a paper, Kirk," Ms. Hogan replied. "For example, you could have gotten ahold of that paper from a friend who has a brother or sister in college."

"But I didn't!" Kirk protested. "I wrote that paper!"

"Since I have no proof, I must do what I said I would do," the teacher said as she handed Kirk the paper. "I have given you an A. Here it is. That should close the matter."

From her tone of voice, Kirk could tell that she still believed he had cheated. She just didn't know how. As he took the paper from her, he trembled with anger.

"No, that doesn't close the matter, Ms. Hogan," he said. "I want an apology."

Ms. Hogan looked startled. "You must be joking," she said. "Surely you realize that when I suspected cheating, I had the responsibility to check into it. When a student's writing ability jumps from a B minus to an A, a teacher has to suspect plagiarism. It wouldn't be fair to the other students if I didn't."

"I've never cheated, Ms. Hogan, and your accusation hurt me a lot," Kirk said. "You had no right to act as if I was guilty before you had proof."

Kirk could tell that he was having no effect on her. She was still regarding him coldly, as if he were lying to her. He *had* to make her understand how she had made him feel. He wanted her to know that part of this ordeal would stay with him forever. And so he added, "I'll *never* forget this, Ms. Hogan!"

Suddenly Kirk saw the same thing he had seen in the coach's eyes and in Ms. Hogan's eyes before—fear. Fear of the black youth who sat before her. She had interpreted Kirk's final words as a threat, something he had not meant them to be.

He started to explain, but then Ms. Hogan said in a trembling voice, "Kirk, I would recommend that you see a counselor about the anger issues you are dealing with. Please send in Letoya."

"Ms. Hogan—" Kirk began again. But he could see it was futile to try to continue the conversation. The teacher had turned her attention to Letoya's paper and acted as if she didn't hear. Kirk got up then and left the office.

"Letoya, you're next," he mumbled as he walked past the table.

"Did she find it, Howell?" Karl called as Kirk walked by. But Kirk ignored him.

When Kirk saw B. J. by the lockers later, B. J. asked what had happened with Ms. Hogan. Kirk sighed and opened his locker. "She couldn't prove I cheated, so I got my A. But I can tell that she still doesn't believe I wrote that paper."

"You're kidding!" B. J. replied.

"And she didn't even say she was sorry," Kirk added, taking out the books for his next class.

B. J. clapped Kirk on the back. "Well, at least you pulled the A you had coming, cuz. Teachers never say they're sorry to students. They don't have to. They've got the power; we don't. But don't waste any time thinking about that woman. She's going to pay—one way or another."

But Kirk didn't hear the menace in B. J.'s voice. He was too upset to notice anything but his own feelings. He had really expected Ms. Hogan to apologize to him once she realized she had misjudged him. But she hadn't been sorry. She had acted as if Kirk really was a cheat, albeit a clever one. As if somehow he had pulled it off, but she simply couldn't prove it.

But what bothered Kirk just as much was the fear he had seen in the teacher's eyes. He hadn't meant for his words to be a threat. But she had interpreted them that way. Like Coach Bromley, Ms. Hogan had so easily assumed that Kirk was capable of hurting her. And all because his skin was black.

Now Kirk could understand why so many young black men joined gangs. If people were instinctively afraid of one young black man, how much more afraid they would be of a whole gang of them!

Many gang members were from poor families. Many had attended dilapidated schools and received substandard educations. Many couldn't afford to go on to college or trade school even if they wanted to. It didn't take them long to figure out that by the time they were old enough to enter the job market, the only jobs they would get were dead-end jobs that no one else wanted.

When they were powerless in so many aspects of their lives, Kirk asked himself, why *wouldn't* they crave the power being in a gang brought them?

* * *

As Kirk was heading out of the building after school, he ran into Karl.

"Hey, did you hear what happened to Ms. Hogan?" Karl asked. "Somebody keyed her car today."

"No kidding?" Kirk asked.

"Yeah, one of the girls in my chemistry class saw it when she was outside during P.E.," Karl replied. "She said there's a big gash that runs the whole length of it. Whoever did it didn't touch the other cars around it. They just zeroed in on that pretty little red Beretta Hogan owns."

Kirk got a rush of adrenaline. Yes! he thought. It's payback time! But just as quickly, he got a sick feeling because he was almost sure he knew who had done it.

"My guess is they'll think it's one of us who had his paper withheld," Karl went on. "I don't suppose you know anything about it, do you, Howell?"

"Me? Um . . . no," Kirk said. "Look, I've got to get going. See you, Karl."

"See you," Karl replied as he headed for his own locker.

A few minutes later, Kirk spotted B. J. "Yo, B. J.," he shouted. "Did you hear what happened to Ms. Hogan's car?"

B. J. smiled. "Didn't I say she was going to pay? Didn't I say there was justice in the world?"

"B. J., you didn't have anything to do with that, did you?" Kirk asked nervously. "I never asked anybody to even the score for me."

"Friends don't have to ask," B. J. said. "Be cool, Howie. Nobody saw a thing."

"B. J., you shouldn't have—" Kirk said.

A hurt look crossed B. J.'s face. "Kirk, you're my brother," he said. "When I see another brother hurting, what am I going to do but even the score?"

Kirk realized then that B. J. had done the deed out of loyalty to him. He grabbed B. J.'s hand in a friendly grip. "It's okay, B. J. You did just fine," he said. "You did just what a brother should do."

* * *

The next morning as Kirk came into the locker room before practice, he heard a familiar voice mention his name. Kirk stopped where he was, still unseen, and listened.

"And Kirk Howell was one of them?" Chad Spencer was asking. "Are you sure?"

Kirk knew Chad was there for swimming practice.

"Yeah," another voice said. "Ms. Hogan busted four kids for getting their reports off the Internet. Isn't Howell that tall black guy you hang out with, Chad?"

"Yeah, but it amazes me that he'd do a stupid thing like turn in a report he downloaded from the Internet," Chad said.

"Well, Hogan caught them because I guess their reports were a lot better than usual," the other guy said, laughing. "She must have figured that people like Howell aren't capable of such good work. Those guys are pretty lazy, you know. They take the easy way out. Just download the stuff."

"Yeah, I guess so," Chad said.

Kirk came around the corner then, surprising both boys. Kirk turned an angry stare on Chad. "You know what, Spencer? I got an A on that paper because Ms. Hogan had to admit that I didn't take my report off the Internet. I did it myself! Thanks for standing up for me when your friend here is putting me down, Chad. Thanks a lot!"

"Kirk, hey, I . . . I never said you cheated," Chad stammered.

"Well, you might as well have," Kirk snapped.

Kirk was angry all morning. He had thought Chad Spencer was his friend. But Chad hadn't even stood up for him when the other guy had said that all black kids were lazy. Chad knew better, yet he had sided with his white friend.

Tucker and B. J. and the other guys were right, Kirk thought. They were all one another had. It was foolish to look for friends outside the hood. They were all fakes. They didn't stick with you, no matter how often you proved yourself worthy. B. J. shouldn't have keyed Ms. Hogan's car, Kirk admitted. But at least he was willing to stick by Kirk, to go out on a limb for him. That was more than Chad Spencer would ever do.

At lunch, Kirk told Deana what had

happened that morning. "I sure found out who my real friends are," Kirk said.

"That's absurd, Kirk," Deana replied. "Just because Chad wimped out like that doesn't mean everybody would have. One of my closest friends is white. The other's Korean. They'd do anything for me. And I'd do anything for them."

"It's not that way with guys," Kirk explained. "You can go to the mall with these girls, but it's all on the surface. With us guys, it runs deeper."

A serious look came to Deana's face. "Kirk, everybody is talking about how Ms. Hogan's car was keyed. You don't know anything about that, do you?"

"You mean did I do it?" Kirk asked angrily.

"Oh, Kirk, you are so touchy lately!" Deana cried. "I'd never think you'd do something like that. But . . . your friends might. I just wondered if you had heard anything."

"If I had, do you think I'd be sitting here talking about it?" Kirk replied. "Whoever did it probably had his reasons, and I'll leave it to the brother's own conscience."

"Oh, so it's okay that somebody scraped a big gouge in the side of Ms. Hogan's car as long as a 'brother' did it?" Deana asked sharply.

Kirk shrugged and said, "I'm not saying anything about it. It's none of my business, okay?"

"Kirk, you're talking more like a gang member every day," Deana said. "I think one of those so-called friends of yours is going to suck you right into that life. They've got you thinking it's all right to do bad things as long as your friends are on your side."

"I pick my friends, and you pick yours, Deana," Kirk said coldly.

"Tucker Chandler is in the Red Princes. If you keep hanging out with him, everybody's going to think you're a Rep too, and you could get shot!" Deana said.

"Tucker's been my friend for most of my life," Kirk said. "I don't plan on turning my back on him any time soon. Where's the loyalty in that?"

"That's pure gang trash talk," Deana said with an angry toss of her head. " 'You stick with your friends no matter what they do.' "

The bell rang then, and Deana stood up. "You know something, Kirk?" she asked. "I don't like what you're becoming."

"Maybe I don't see the world the same way you do, Deana," Kirk said. "Maybe I remember where I came from more than you do."

"What's that supposed to mean?" Deana demanded.

"You're a sister, Deana, but you act more like those girls you hang out with," Kirk replied. "You don't spend time with your old friends anymore."

"Addie and Melissa were my friends in middle school. They were both black. But Addie moved to Florida, and Melissa's a gang girl now. So excuse me if I'd rather spend my time with people who have the same interests and goals I have," Deana said.

"Well, Deana, maybe it's just easier for you to forget people. But I'm sticking with my old friends," Kirk said.

Deana picked up her tray and stomped off without another word.

Boy, Kirk thought to himself, is she ever acting white! He understood now what his friends were trying to tell him when they accused him of that. It was like acting as if everything in your past was inferior. It was as if being important and popular meant having only white friends. Worst of all, it meant avoiding many of your old friends, as if you might catch the disease of failure from them.

I'm never going to be that way, Kirk resolved. Never.

8 The next day in algebra, Mr. Ha asked Kirk if he could see him after class.

Kirk was startled. What was this about? he wondered. When Ms. Hogan had asked to see him after class, it was to accuse him of cheating. Was something wrong in algebra now too? Maybe Mr. Ha had heard the gossip about Kirk being a cheat. Maybe he wanted to warn Kirk about cheating in algebra. Or perhaps someone had told Mr. Ha that Kirk had probably been the culprit in the incident involving Ms. Hogan's car. Maybe Mr. Ha would try and convict him just as Ms. Hogan had done—without any proof.

Kirk sighed. He liked Mr. Ha and had always thought Mr. Ha liked him. But Kirk was learning very quickly that appearances can be deceiving. It wouldn't surprise him if the math teacher stabbed him in the back just as everyone else seemed to be doing lately.

When class was over, Kirk approached Mr. Ha's desk after the rest of the students had filed out.

"Kirk," Mr. Ha began, "is everything okay with you?"

"Yeah, sure," Kirk said.

"You have seemed ah . . . preoccupied lately," Mr. Ha added.

"Sorry. Guess I just have a few things on my mind," Kirk mumbled.

"Kirk, you are my best student, my most promising student," the soft-spoken teacher continued. "I am delighted by the way you love mathematics. You remind me of my son when he was your age."

"Thanks," Kirk said. Suddenly he was ashamed of the negative thoughts he had just had about the teacher.

Mr. Ha smiled. "I'm sure you're wondering why I wanted to talk to you. Well, I'm hoping to start a tutoring program for students who struggle with math. And I was wondering if you might be available for perhaps two hours one afternoon a week. I think you might be able to reach some of the students I can't. You would, of course, get academic credit for your participation. And it would look good on your scholarship applications."

Kirk's first reaction was to jump at the chance to participate in such a project. But his enthusiasm waned when he remembered what Ms. Hogan had done to him. Kirk was angry at the whole school for allowing something like that to happen. "Um . . . well . . ." Kirk said.

"Please think about it, Kirk," Mr. Ha said. "Then give me your decision. I know you are very busy with your difficult schedule and your job. But I would be so grateful if you could do this for the sake of the other students. Those who don't have your knack for math."

"Okay, I'll let you know," Kirk said, leaving the classroom.

"Why would you want to take on more work?" B. J. demanded when Kirk told him what Mr. Ha had proposed. "There's no money in it."

"No, but it'd look good on my academic record," Kirk said.

B. J. shook his head. "Beats me why anyone would want to do a lot of extra work for nothing," he said. Then he perked up. "Hey, some of the guys are throwing a party for an old homie who's coming back to the hood. You want to come? It's Friday night."

"Who's the party for?" Kirk asked.

"You remember Duff Freebold?" B. J. asked.

"Oh, yeah. He played baseball with Garrison when we were freshmen," Kirk said. "He always said he was going to be another Tony Gwynn because he practiced like Gwynn did as a kid. He hit figs instead of baseballs. I haven't seen Duff in a long time. Not since . . ." Kirk's voice trailed off.

When Duff Freebold had been a senior at Garrison, he got mixed up in a liquor store robbery. He was a gang wanna-be back then. And he went along with whatever the older guys did.

"Duff was framed, you know," B. J. said. "That whole trial was a setup. Another guy who was in the liquor store at the time lied and said Duff was there. That guy was in with the Twelfth Avenue crowd. Duff's been through a lot. Going to the lockup when he didn't do anything. That's why we need to give him a big welcome home so he knows his friends are still with him. So, are you going? Tuck'll be there."

"Okay, sure," Kirk said. Kirk liked parties in general, so he didn't mind going. But he remembered Duff as a loudmouthed braggart who happened to be an adept batter. He might have even taken the Falcons to the city championship if he hadn't been busted for taking down that liquor store. But Duff was never serious enough about baseball to be great like Gwynn.

Kirk remembered one day in particular when the Falcons were practicing. Everyone else on the team had been hustling, but Duff was constantly stopping to shoot the breeze with friends who were watching practice. Kirk was standing nearby, and he heard Duff say, "Coach Wedloe is a fool. How come he's always yelling at me when I'm the only one on this team who can play decent ball?"

"Coach just wants us all to practice, Duff," Kirk had pointed out good-naturedly. "He wants us to be prepared for the next game. It'll be a tough one."

Instantly, Duff came over and yelled into Kirk's face, "I don't *need* to practice, you little weirdo. What do you know about baseball? You're a *freshman!*"

Kirk had been surprised at how hostile Duff had become.

"Even Tony Gwynn practices," Kirk had said under his breath as he walked away from Duff that day. He didn't think Duff had heard the remark, but later on, he found out that Duff had heard it.

As Tucker, Kirk, and B. J. were walking home from practice that afternoon, a car full of seniors cruised by. Duff hung out the side window and yelled, "Hey, Howell. You're always talking about Tony Gwynn. How'd you like one of his signed baseballs?"

"You mean it?" Kirk had gasped. But he couldn't help wondering why Duff was doing something so nice for him.

"Sure, kid," Duff said. "Be out in your yard about 6:00 tonight. I'll swing by and give it to you."

"You got it, man!" Kirk exclaimed. As the Mazda spun away, Kirk could hardly believe his good fortune. Why had Duff picked him? he wondered. Why not Tucker or B. J.?

Kirk waited outside his house that evening, and the Mazda appeared at 6:00 sharp. Kirk could see Duff in the passenger seat and a couple of other guys in the backseat.

"Catch, kid," Duff shouted as they drove by. He pitched an object out the window. Kirk was prepared to catch the treasure, and he did. But it wasn't a baseball signed by Tony Gwynn. It was a very rotten tomato, and it dripped off Kirk's hands and onto his shoes.

The Mazda made a wild U-turn then. As it drove by, Kirk could hear laughter spilling out the windows.

Now Kirk was supposed to go to Duff's welcome-home party? Well, maybe Duff wasn't the same guy anymore, Kirk thought. Besides, the Freebolds were a nice family. They were hardworking people. When Kirk's dad had been out of work one year, the Freebolds invited them over for a big turkey dinner on Christmas. There were even gifts under the tree for seven-year-old Kirk and little Kandace.

So, Kirk reasoned, he would go to the party out of respect for Duff's family.

When Friday night came, Tucker picked up Kirk and B. J. in his fancy car. "We're going to this party in style," Tucker boasted on the way.

As the three entered the house where the party was being held, Kirk spotted Duff standing by a table of food. Right away Kirk noticed that Duff looked different. He had always been a little overweight before, but now he was lean and hard-bodied. His face had aged in a startling way. The flesh seemed to have melted away from his bones, giving him a gaunt look. Duff was about 21, but he could have passed for 31.

"Hey, Tucker, my man!" Duff shouted. He and Tucker had been pretty close before Duff went away to jail. Tucker had always worshipped Duff. And now when Kirk looked at Tucker's face, he could see that the situation hadn't changed.

"Duff, how've you been?" Tucker asked in an awed voice. As if Duff were a New York Yankees hitter instead of an ex-con.

"Prime, brother, prime," Duff replied, smiling broadly.

The house was crowded and jumping with hip-hop music. Kirk noticed that most of the guys there were members of the Red Princes.

"What was it like up there at the camp,

man?" Tucker asked Duff. Kirk thought Tucker looked like a little kid waiting for a battle-scarred hero to tell his war stories.

"I was boss," Duff said simply. "I took over. Even the guards were afraid of me."

"All right!" Tucker cried, giving Duff a high five.

"But it wasn't any fun being locked up," Duff continued. "Wasn't right that Duff Freebold was in a cage just because some yellow dog from Twelfth Avenue lied about what happened."

A solemn mood descended then. Everyone grew silent.

"Marco Lyman was the one who fingered me," Duff said. "Swore I was in that store, but I wasn't. He did it because his younger brother and me had it out one night. I busted the kid's arm, but he had it coming."

Kirk wasn't so sure that Lyman hadn't been telling the truth. Duff was hanging out with older guys who had hit several liquor stores in the area. It seemed plausible he was with them that night too—the night a lady clerk was shot.

But now everybody sided with Duff.

"Marco's working at the convenience store over on Walnut now," B. J. said.

"Well, I'm not forgetting the score I have with him and his friends over on Twelfth Avenue," Duff said.

Kirk shared his suspicions with Tucker and B. J. when they rode home that night.

"You know, that lady who was shot at the liquor store lost the use of her right arm. I heard it changed her whole life," Kirk said. "Duff was always hanging around with those guys who robbed those other stores. How do we know Marco was lying when he said he saw Duff that night?"

"I can't believe what I'm hearing," Tucker said. "Duff is a brother. The Twelfth Avenue guys are our enemies. They've always been trying to walk all over the Reps."

"Yeah, Howie," B. J. said, "now you're talking like you're not a brother again!"

Suddenly Tucker turned a corner and pulled the car up to a curb on a dark street.

"We need to talk," Tucker said, turning around to look Kirk in the eye. "We've got to get something straight. Are you a brother or aren't you?"

"Look," Kirk said, "all I'm saying is, maybe Duff Freebold wasn't framed."

"*You* are caving in, man," Tucker said. "You're sounding as if you're not on our side anymore, on the Red Princes' side. You sound as if you're siding with the Twelfth Avenue rats even though they framed a brother. Now you listen up, Howie. We want to know where you stand."

"We've always been friends, you guys," Kirk said a little nervously. "You know that."

"Are you on the side of the Reps or not?" Tucker demanded. "If you're not with us, heart and soul, maybe you'll go warn Marco Lyman that we're looking for payback. Then maybe the Twelfth Avenue guys will get a shooting party together and get us before we get them."

Kirk felt the perspiration breaking out on his body. "I'm on your side, man. You know I am," he said.

"Then join us Reps," B. J. said.

"*Us?*" Kirk repeated, feeling his heart sink. "You joined, B. J.?"

"Yep, yesterday," B. J. said proudly.

"That's right," Tucker said. "And that only leaves you, Howie."

"I don't know . . ." Kirk said.

"Let me put it this way," Tucker said in an ominous voice. "Throw in with the Reps, or we're finished with you. All the other brothers will freeze you out too. We got ways of spreading the word that you're a narc, Kirk. Yeah, no one will have anything to do with you. You're going to feel so alone, you'll think you were dropped at the South Pole."

"And your white friends won't hang with you either," B. J. added. "From what I heard, most of them think you're a cheat."

Tucker reached into a bag in the backseat then and took out a polo shirt with a red collar. "The teachers at Garrison won't let the Reps wear their colors in bandannas. But they're too stupid to recognize the colors in the collar of a polo shirt. The Reps will know though. We want you to be wearing this shirt at school on Monday, Howie. You show the Reps' colors, or you're slime. You hear what I'm saying?"

Tucker dropped the shirt in Kirk's lap. Then, in silence, he drove Kirk home.

"Remember," Tucker said as Kirk got

out of the car. "You show your colors
Monday, or you just threw away your
friendship with every guy you ever knew
in the hood."

9 Kirk was still so confused and nervous that he almost forgot about basketball practice on Saturday morning. By the time he arrived, the other players were already headed out of the locker room, dressed and ready to practice. Kirk changed quickly and then sprinted up the stairs to the gymnasium.

"Hey, Kirk," Ross Dittman said in greeting as Kirk ran onto the floor.

"Hi, Ross," Kirk said.

Ross was the talented center of the team, and Kirk had a lot of respect for him. But he'd heard that Ross was on the verge of being disqualified because of his grades.

Coach Bromley started to reprimand Kirk when he saw him come onto the court late. But then he abruptly turned away. Kirk figured it was because the coach was still hesitant to cross him after their last confrontation.

Toward the end of the practice session, Kirk was surprised to see Mr. Ha come in and sit in the bleachers. He had never come to any of the practices before, and Kirk noticed that he seemed to be watching him closely.

The team practiced for 90 minutes as usual. Then they headed for the showers. When Kirk emerged from the locker room in his street clothes, Mr. Ha was waiting for him.

"Kirk, forgive me for intruding on your time during the weekend, but I had to talk to you again," Mr. Ha said.

Kirk was in no mood to talk to anybody right now. Before Monday morning he had to decide if he would wear gang colors or lose all his friends.

"Perhaps we could go across the street to the coffee shop," Mr. Ha suggested. "I'll buy you a cold soda. You must be thirsty after that practice."

"Okay," Kirk shrugged.

When they were sitting in the coffee shop, Mr. Ha said, "I already spoke to you about the tutoring program, Kirk. I don't know if I told you how desperately some of the students need this. This could be the last chance for some of them to grasp math. Have you given any more thought to participating?"

"Well, I've been kind of busy," Kirk said.

"I understand," Mr. Ha replied. "But if I may, let me share something personal, Kirk.

I have had many fine students, but only a few have had an intense love for the subject. My son, Justin, did. He was a student much like you. And like you, his goal was to become an engineer. He tutored others in high school. And he made a big difference for about a dozen students. They graduated because of him and went on to good jobs."

"Did your son go on to become an engineer?" Kirk asked.

"He started to," the teacher replied, taking on a look of sadness. "But he never finished college."

"Why not?" Kirk wanted to know.

Mr. Ha sighed deeply. "In his freshman year, he was diagnosed with leukemia," he said. "A few months later, he . . . returned to his ancestors."

"Oh," Kirk said, startled. "I'm sorry."

"Yes, thank you," Mr. Ha said, nodding his head. "But the reason I mention this is because you have the spark of genius Justin had. You are almost like a second son to me, Kirk. When you explain a problem in class, many understand the concept for the first time. Those students need someone like you so very much."

Kirk was touched by the teacher's words. "Can I let you know on Monday?" he asked.

"That would be fine," Mr. Ha replied. "Thank you, Kirk."

"You're welcome, Mr. Ha," Kirk answered. He watched the small, round-shouldered, balding man walk away.

Kirk shook his head, thinking what an amazing person the teacher was. He had suffered the death of a brilliant son, and yet he still had such compassion for the students who struggled. And he had treated Kirk with so much respect. Mr. Ha—who held a Ph.D. in math from Cal Tech—who continued to teach at an inner-city high school because he thought he was most needed there—had treated a 17-year-old black kid from the hood as he would treat a valued colleague!

Kirk spent most of the rest of the weekend working at the hot dog stand. He didn't tell his parents about the choice facing him on Monday. It would just worry them. And what could they do about it anyway? It was a choice Kirk had to make alone.

Kirk didn't tell his parents about Mr. Ha's tutoring project either. He wasn't sure he could handle it if he lost all his friends at Garrison. Every time Kirk would walk down the halls at school, they'd find ways to hassle him. He'd seen it done to others before. How would he be able to concentrate on his own schoolwork, much less tutor others?

Kirk kept going back and forth in his mind about what to do on Monday. He remembered all the good times he'd had with Tucker and B. J. and the other guys. He could hardly imagine what life would be like without them. No one to hang out with anymore. No one to go to parties with, rap with . . .

And who would be left? Chad Spencer had already made it clear where he stood. He was all too ready to believe that Kirk was a cheat. Let's face it, Kirk thought miserably, if his old friends ostracized him, he'd be a total outcast.

At home on Sunday night, Kirk pulled down the Garrison yearbook from his freshman year. Justin Ha had been a senior that year. Freshmen, like Kirk, had paid little attention to seniors, but everybody knew the Chinese kid who won all the academic awards. Justin had graduated with honors and was the valedictorian for his class. Then, just a little while later, as his father had sadly said, he returned to his ancestors.

Kirk shook his head again as he thought about Mr. Ha. How bravely he had gone on teaching while he must have been coping with his son's illness and death. How bravely he had gone on in the face of such a profound tragedy. When his own heart was breaking, he agonized over the students who were falling behind. And now he had reached out to Kirk to help save them. What a great heart the man had.

* * *

On Monday morning Kirk picked up the polo shirt from the chair where it had hung since Friday night. That's what they're expecting me to wear today, he told himself. The colors. The Reps' colors.

Kirk sat down on the bed and thought about what it would be like to be in a gang. No doubt it would be exciting. And it would be a way of getting respect. But, for Kirk, probably the biggest draw was the camaraderie of the gang. Like being a soldier in a war when you risk your very life for your comrades. Kirk hungered for that feeling of belonging, that feeling of brotherhood.

He considered putting on the shirt. He rationalized that just wearing the polo shirt wouldn't be like actually *being* a Red Prince. It would just be like throwing a bone to his friends, appeasing them. It really wouldn't mean that much. Maybe he wouldn't have to ride with them or join them in their gang activities. Maybe once he wore the shirt, they'd be satisfied. Everything would be cool again. And he could get on with his life.

Besides, how could he refuse? It would mean turning his back on his friends. And Kirk couldn't do that. Kirk was afraid to do that. He had to wear the shirt, and that's all there was to it. He had no choice.

But Kirk's hands shook as he held up

the polo shirt and prepared to pull it over his head. And suddenly, for no apparent reason, the image of Mr. Ha came into his mind. Kirk thought of the man teaching his mathematics classes while his son was fighting his last, losing battle. What courage that must have taken. Then Kirk thought about his mother, rising each morning to face another day of pain. Struggling to maintain a normal life—for herself and for her family—in the face of a crippling disease. What courage she must have. Much more courage than refusing to wear a stupid shirt with a red collar . . .

When Kirk came out for breakfast, the eggs and browned sausages already lay on his plate. Mom's timing is always perfect, Kirk thought, smiling and taking his place at the table.

Mrs. Howell wheeled herself to the table and set out the syrup for pancakes. She gave Kirk a big smile.

"Good morning, sweetie," she said. "Did you sleep well?"

"Yeah, sure," Kirk lied. He had awakened several times during the night, torn about his decision.

"I heard you get up twice," Kandace said. "You woke me up both times."

His mother looked at him with concern.

"Something wrong, Kirk?" she asked as she passed him the pancakes.

"Um . . . I couldn't sleep because I have a decision to make today," Kirk replied.

"Oh? What kind of decision?" his mother wanted to know.

Kirk hesitated a moment before answering. He couldn't tell them about the decision he had to make concerning the Reps. So he said, "Mr. Ha wants me to spend two hours a week tutoring some kids in math."

"Oh, Kirk," Mrs. Howell said, "that would be wonderful! You know, I ran into Mrs. Dittman the other day at the grocery store. She's so worried because Ross is floundering in math. Maybe you could help him."

"Maybe," Kirk said.

"I bet you'd be good at tutoring," Kandace said. "I know you always help me when I can't figure out some problem."

"Well, I'm supposed to decide today," Kirk said. "I guess I'll go ahead and do it."

"Oh, good," Mom said. "I've always

been proud of you for being so smart and so helpful. But I don't think I've *ever* been as proud of you as I am now."

"Thanks, Mom," Kirk said.

"Hey, Kirk, why are you wearing that shirt?" Kandace asked.

"What's wrong with my shirt?" Kirk replied.

"Nothing," Kandace said with a shrug. "But it's not even baseball season. I just wondered why you were wearing that old Tony Gwynn T-shirt now. It's so faded."

Kirk smiled. "It might be old and faded, but it works all right for me this morning."

He finished his breakfast then and hiked on his backpack. But as he headed out to his car, a feeling of dread set in. He couldn't remember a time when he had been less anxious to go to school.

10

The first person Kirk met as he walked into Garrison High that morning was Roell.

"Man, you're a turncoat," Roell hissed as he walked by.

Kirk walked on, ignoring him. Worse things awaited him, he knew. When he walked into math he'd have to confront B. J.

As Kirk entered Mr. Ha's classroom, B. J. looked up from his conversation with Roell and Desmond. B. J.'s look sliced through Kirk like a knife.

Kirk looked at the clock. Mr. Ha would not arrive for a few more minutes, so they had plenty of time to harass him. He braced himself.

"Anybody smell something *foul* in here?" B. J. asked in a loud voice.

"Stinks worse than garbage," Roell said. "Garbage that's been sitting in the sun too long."

Kirk opened his book and tried to ignore the remarks.

"Hey, Roell, what do you do with a brother who turns on you?" B. J. asked.

"Seems to me like we can do anything

we want—starting *now*," Roell replied, menace coming through in his voice.

Kirk continued to stare at his book. But the words and equations weren't registering in his mind. He might as well have been looking at a blank page.

Just then Mr. Ha walked in, and the three quieted down for a few minutes. But as soon as the lesson began, they started up again. For the rest of the period, the three made remarks filled with underlying threats. Kirk sighed. I might as well get used to it, he told himself. Because this is the way it's going to be.

After class, Kirk told Mr. Ha that he would take the tutoring job.

"I am so pleased," Mr. Ha said. He took Kirk to the math resource room, where there were several computers and desks. He explained that the next day Kirk would begin his tutoring duties in that room. The class would consist of four students, including Ross Dittman.

As Kirk walked toward English, he saw Deana. She walked by him without saying a word. He couldn't blame her for being mad at him after the way he'd talked to her. But he hurried ahead and touched her on the shoulder.

She turned and said icily, "What do you want?"

"I just wanted to tell you that I'm sorry," Kirk said. "About the way I acted, I mean." Then before she could turn away, he told her about his decision not to wear the Reps' colors that day.

"They all hate me now that I didn't do it," he said. "I don't know for sure what kind of trouble I'm in, but I know I feel like I've lost half of myself."

Deana smiled a forgiving smile then and said, "You did the right thing, Kirk."

"Easy to say, Deana," Kirk said sadly. "I've already been getting hate looks. I can't believe they've all turned on me."

"I can," Deanna said. "It's one for all and all for one in those gangs. Anybody who goes against that gets shunned. They don't allow any room for individuality."

"Well, talk to you later, okay?" Kirk said. "I've got to get to English before the bell rings."

"Sure," Deana replied. "I'll meet you at lunch."

Kirk got to English just before the bell rang. He was surprised when Ms. Hogan called him to her desk and asked him to come into her office after class for a third time. Now what's *this* about? he wondered with a sigh. I suppose she's going to accuse me of keying her car.

"Kirk, sit down," Ms. Hogan said as Kirk entered her office after class. "I think we need to talk."

Kirk sat down in the same chair he had sat in before.

"Kirk, I'm going to come right to the point," the teacher began. "Did you vandalize my car? As a way of getting back at me for the paper incident?"

"No," Kirk said. "I didn't."

Ms. Hogan stared at him hard for a moment. Then she said, "All right, I believe you. You can go now."

Kirk was confused. She believed him? Why? She hadn't believed him before.

"I don't understand," Kirk said. "Why do you believe me now?"

"I was talking to Mr. Ha the other day," she replied. "He told me how determined you are to make something of yourself. He said he had never seen anyone work harder or improve more in his class. Based on what Mr. Ha told me, I think I misjudged you. I've decided that you were telling the truth about writing your paper. So I have no reason to doubt you now. You're dismissed."

Kirk stood up to leave.

"Wait, Kirk," the teacher added. "Before you go, I think I owe you something."

Kirk frowned. "Owe me something?" he asked.

"I know it's a little late in coming, but I apologize," Ms. Hogan said. "For accusing you of cheating."

Kirk remained silent. He was skeptical. Why would Ms. Hogan apologize to him now? he wondered. And was she being sincere?

"I was just doing my job, Kirk," the teacher went on. "I've had many cheaters in the past, some I've caught and some I haven't. But every time a student gets by with cheating, it's unfair to the other students. The students who work hard for their grades. And so I'm probably a little harder on those I suspect of cheating than

I should be. That doesn't make me very popular, I know. But I'm not here to win a popularity contest. I'm here to teach. To do everything in my power to ensure that my students leave my classroom prepared. That's my job. And if that means not being everyone's favorite teacher, then so be it. Can you understand that, Kirk?"

"I don't know," Kirk said. "I understand the part about wanting to be a good teacher, but . . ." He hesitated.

"But what, Kirk?" Ms. Hogan pressed.

"But why does that have to include denying that you're . . . black?" Kirk asked. "Acting white, I mean."

Ms. Hogan sighed. "Kirk, I'm not acting white *or* black. I'm not acting at all. I'm just being me. Just because I don't pal around with the black students doesn't mean I'm denying my heritage. Do you see me palling around with the white students?"

"No," Kirk admitted. "It just seems that you favor white students. As if you think black students aren't very smart. Like when you accused me of not writing my paper because you thought I wasn't capable of it."

"Kirk, let me ask you something," the teacher said. "Of the four students whose papers I withheld, how many were black?"

"Two," Kirk said.

"And how many were white?" Ms. Hogan pressed.

"Two," Kirk replied.

"Is that showing favoritism to the white students?" the teacher asked.

"I guess not," Kirk said. He hadn't thought of that.

"Why does a person have to *act* like anything?" Ms. Hogan wanted to know. "Do you know what Emerson meant when he said, 'Imitation is suicide,' Kirk?"

"No," Kirk said. He'd seen the quotation on a poster in Ms. Hogan's classroom but had really never thought much about it.

"Emerson meant that by acting like someone else, you kill a part of yourself— of your own individuality. Your own uniqueness. I've always tried not to do that," Ms. Hogan said. "I simply try to be myself. Some people interpret that as denying my heritage. Others interpret it as arrogance. But it's neither. I'm just trying to be me."

"Can I ask you something, Ms. Hogan?" Kirk wanted to know.

"All right," the teacher replied. "I guess that's only fair."

"Are you afraid of me because I'm black?" Kirk asked.

Ms. Hogan hesitated before answering. Then she said, "Not because you're black, Kirk," she said. "But I've seen the group you hang out with. I know they're your friends, but I also know that some of them associate with a gang. And that's what scares me. If they're your friends, who's to say you don't act like them when you're not in my classroom? I had a cousin who was killed by a gang in a drive-by shooting. They mistook him for one of their rivals. I know how dangerous gangs can be, Kirk. And I'm afraid that again I misjudged you. And for that I apologize as well."

* * *

At lunchtime, none of the usuals came to join Kirk at his table. Kirk could see them at the other end of the cafeteria, as far from him as possible. They were laughing and having a good time, and Kirk wished he were among them. He looked around for Deana but didn't see her.

Then, suddenly, Ross Dittman appeared with his tray. "Anybody sitting here?" he asked.

"No, nobody," Kirk said.

"I'll sure be glad to get some help with algebra," Ross said as he sat down and cracked open a carton of chocolate milk. "Mr. Ha has tried to help me, but I just don't get it. Maybe I'm just stupid." He took a huge gulp of milk.

"That's not it at all," Kirk said. "Math just isn't your strong suit, just like English isn't mine. But I'm amazed at how you pile up points in the games. We all have our strengths and our weaknesses, Ross."

Ross grinned a little, but then he quickly added, "Yeah, but basketball's probably never going to take me anywhere. I do all right on the court, but I'm no Michael Jordan. I need to graduate so I can get a decent job. I want to major in business administration at the community college if I can. I'd like to own a sporting goods store someday."

"Sounds good," Kirk said. "You probably will."

* * *

Kirk had his first tutoring session with Ross and the others the next day. By the end of the session, he felt as if he'd really helped them. They all seemed to better understand the concept they were having problems with.

He left the session feeling good about himself and wondered why he hadn't made more of an attempt in the past to become friends with Ross Dittman. He was a nice guy. But Kirk had always been too busy with Tucker and B. J. Kirk sighed. Maybe he and Ross *would* become friends since he would no longer be hanging out with the others.

All week long, Kirk was barraged with hate looks and insults. Twice he was jammed against the lockers by an attack from behind. Then, the sides of his old Mercury were gouged with a key, and two tires were flat one day when he went to leave school. But despite what was going on, Kirk found himself yearning to be with his old friends again. He missed playing basketball with them and cruising the hood on Saturday night.

By the end of the week, the word was on the street that the Red Princes and the Twelfth Avenue gang were going to fight it out that weekend. Duff Freebold meant to settle the score with Marco Lyman.

When Kirk heard about the upcoming battle, he was sick with worry. More often than not, gang fights involved guns. And Kirk didn't think he could stand it if one of his friends was shot, even though they had turned against him.

He tried calling B. J., but B. J. cursed him and hung up. And Tucker told him to drop dead before slamming down the receiver in Kirk's ear.

Saturday night, Kirk was sitting at home alone, missing his friends and worrying about them more than ever. Deana was at a sleepover, so he couldn't even get his mind off his troubles by being with her. He had decided to put together some kind of lesson plan for his next tutoring session, but he was failing miserably. About 10:00, he decided to go out for a walk. He told himself that the fresh air would do him good. But the real reason he was leaving was to head over to Twelfth Avenue to see if anything had taken place between the two gangs. He had to make sure his friends were all right. Then he could return to his work.

A police car roared by Kirk as he rounded the corner onto Twelfth Avenue, and he felt his stomach tighten. Looking ahead, he could see a cluster of cruisers, their red lights throbbing in the darkness. A crowd was gathering. Kirk hurried to the scene, his eyes searching frantically for Tucker's Prelude.

"What happened?" Kirk asked a girl standing on the edge of the crowd.

"Some guys in a drive-by," she said matter-of-factly.

"Was anybody hurt?" Kirk asked tensely.

Two ambulances came screaming up in answer to his question. Kirk saw the Prelude then. The side windows were cracked in spider web patterns. In the center of the cracked glass were little round holes where the bullets had gone in.

"Medical examiner," a nearby onlooker announced as the coroner's van pulled up.

Somebody was dead.

Seconds later, Kirk spotted the face of a kid they were wheeling on a gurney toward the ambulance. His face was streaked with blood, but Kirk recognized him immediately. It was B. J. Kirk felt his insides go cold as he watched his friend being put into the ambulance.

"Who got killed?" the girl next to Kirk asked another bystander.

"Some guy named Chandler. Tucker Chandler," was the response. "Someone said he was a Rep."

The contents of Kirk's stomach rose within him then like lava in a volcano. Clasping his hand to his mouth, he stumbled into an alley and vomited behind a dumpster. And then he cried. All the memories of his friends flashed through his mind like scenes from a movie he'd never see again. Even though it was the best movie he'd ever been to.

* * *

The details were in the newspaper the next day. Duff, Tucker, and B. J. had gone to Twelfth Avenue for a showdown with Marco Lyman and his friends. Duff opened fire on a bunch of Twelfth Avenue guys just getting out of a car. One of the Raiders was seriously injured. The Raiders blasted back. Tucker was killed instantly, and B. J. was injured. Duff escaped unscathed, but he was being held for attempted murder.

But the police found something else at the scene. In Tucker's trunk was several thousand dollars' worth of stolen jewelry. Police speculated that they had found the person who had recently broken into two jewelry stores in the area.

Three days later, Kirk attended Tucker's funeral. Tucker's grandmother, the one who had refused to take him in, was in the front row of the church. She kissed his still face as he lay in the casket lined with white silk.

Such a waste, Kirk told himself as he left the cemetery. He had never felt so sad and alone in his life. He wondered how B. J. was dealing with Tucker's death. He longed to talk to B. J., to find some comfort in his smile, the grasp of his hand. But B. J. was still in the hospital, recovering from a gunshot wound to the side of his head. And even if he weren't, Kirk reminded himself that B. J. now considered him his enemy.

* * *

Two weeks later, B. J. was released from the hospital. Since he hadn't had a gun that night, he wasn't charged in the drive-by shooting. But he had to do some community service and take counseling.

Kirk tried to talk to him a couple of times in algebra class, but B. J. turned away.

Then one Tuesday afternoon, Kirk noticed his former friend standing in the hall outside the math resource room.

Kirk left the four classmates working on an equation and headed out into the hall. He steeled himself for another bitter rejection.

"Hey, B. J., want to crunch some

numbers with us?" he asked softly. "You're probably a little behind . . . after being gone, I mean."

B. J. didn't move. His back was turned. Then, very slowly, he turned toward Kirk. He still wore a bandage on the side of his head where he had been grazed by the bullet.

"My old man made me leave the Reps," B. J. said. "He says I've got one more chance to bring up my grades. If I don't, he's going to send me away to one of those schools that are like boot camps. I don't know if I can do it . . ."

"Sure you can, B. J.," Kirk assured him. "You can do it. I'll help you. Come on."

Hesitantly, B. J. followed Kirk into the resource room. Kirk pulled up a chair for him in front of an empty computer. B. J. sat down, and Kirk pulled up another chair and sat beside him.

For a moment the two sat without speaking. Then B. J. whispered. "He shouldn't have died, Howie. Tuck shouldn't have died."

"No," Kirk answered. "He shouldn't have. I miss him a lot."

"So do I," B. J. said, biting his lip as if to hold back tears. "We were brothers, all three of us."

"You and I still can be," Kirk said, risking a smile.

B. J. didn't reply, so Kirk laid a hand on his shoulder. "Welcome back, brother," he whispered in a shaky voice.

B. J. looked up then with the ghost of a smile on his face. "Back at you, bro'," he said.

PASSAGES Novels by Anne Schraff

An Alien Spring
The Boy from Planet Nowhere
Bridge to the Moon
The Darkest Secret
Don't Blame the Children
The Ghost Boy
Gingerbread Heart
The Haunting of Hawthorne
The Hyena Laughs at Night
Just Another Name for Lonely
Maitland's Kid
Memories Are Forever
Please Don't Ask Me to Love You
The Power of the Rose
The Shadow Man
The Shining Mark
A Song to Sing
Sparrow's Treasure
Summer of Shame
To Slay the Dragon
The Vandal
When a Hero Dies